SLAUGHTER IN THE SUN

Stephen Christie

Set against the glittering, exotic backdrop of lush and tropic Ceylon, this is the story of a case of mystery and of murder which taxed the ability, the ingenuity and the courage of Sexton Blake to the utmost. An original Sexton Blake novel—never before published anywhere in the world in any form—it cannot but win many new readers to swell the ranks of the millions of people all the world over who have thrilled to the exploits of the renowned Baker Street detective for more than seventy-five years.

Other Thrilling
SEXTON BLAKE NOVELS
in this World-Renowned Series

DRIVEN TO KILL
Rex Dolphin

The First Sexton Blake Omnibus
The Second Sexton Blake Omnibus
The Third Sexton Blake Omnibus
The Fourth Sexton Blake Omnibus
The Fifth Sexton Blake Omnibus
The Sixth Sexton Blake Omnibus
The Seventh Sexton Blake Omnibus

All Howard Baker Books

Stephen Christie

SLAUGHTER IN THE SUN

HOWARD BAKER
London

Stephen Christie

SLAUGHTER IN THE SUN

© Press Editorial Services, 1969

An Original Sexton Blake Novel

First publication 1969

A HOWARD BAKER BOOK

SBN 09 300140 1

Howard Baker Books are published by
HOWARD BAKER PUBLISHERS LIMITED
47 Museum Street, London W.C.1
Printed and bound in the United Kingdom by
Balding & Mansell Ltd, of London and Wisbech

SLAUGHTER IN THE SUN

CHAPTER I

So Naked and So Dead

Think thou and act: tomorrow thou shalt die
Outstretched in the sun's warmth upon the shore.
Dante Gabriel Rossetti: *The House of Life*

"AND NOW," said Emily Syms despairingly, "for the last time."

She seated herself at the piano and struck a chord.

At least she meant it to be a chord, but the result jarred even her insensitive listeners.

There were guffaws from the group of teenagers behind her.

Miss Syms pursed her thin lips, peered at the score (which she knew from memory, anyway) and decided to skip the preliminaries.

"Now, children," she beseeched.

The voices burst forth more or less simultaneously into song. Miss Syms played on gamely. The voices drowned even the ceaseless roar of the sea behind the little schoolroom.

For once Emily Syms made no attempt to keep the voices under control. She was not feeling up to it. The headache with which she had got up in the morning had not been made any better by her earlier attempts to discipline her choir. She had, in fact, toyed with the idea of staying back at home and sharing the luxury of invalidism with her sister, Bella.

But Emily Syms had decided to come. For one thing, she was very conscientious. And for another, she had known that she couldn't afford to be ill at the same time as Bella. Bella would always be demanding attention.

7

Her fingers fluttered over the ivories automatically. It was an old piece she was playing, one which brought back memories of days and nights under warm Italian skies—and the bitter event of one night that had, in its eternity, ruined her life.

> '*I love to ride a ferry,*
> *Where music is so merry . . .*'

The words opened the floodgates of memory.

> '*Where boys and girls are dancing,*
> *Where sweethearts go romancing . . .*'

Behind her old-fashioned, gold-rimmed spectacles Emily Syms's eyes grew misty. There would be no romance for her. Not ever. Not after that night. True, they had soon afterwards sold their flourishing little farm near Naples and returned to where they had been born, but the memory would not be left behind. Now there still were blue skies over her, but they were the blazing blue skies of Ceylon and the sea that raged restlessly nearby did not have the blue of the Tyrrhenian but the turgid green of the Indian Ocean.

> '*Life is like a muddy ground—*'

Abruptly her fingers stopped caressing the keyboard.

"Please!" she smiled. "Not 'muddy ground' It's '*mardi gras*'. Mah-di grah."

"What's mardi grah, miss," a piping male voice asked.

Miss Syms closed her eyes in anguish. Such ignorance, she thought. Why, in her time they did not have to explain such a word to any self-respecting teenager—and all teenagers in her time were self-respecting. Of course, in those days they read worthwhile books, not cheap comics. She opened her mouth to explain.

"Please, miss—"

"Yes, what is it, Judy?" She felt another stab of pain at her temples and momentarily closed her eyes again. When she opened them the girl who had spoken was making a significant gesture. The other girls were suppressing giggles. The boys wore wide grins. Miss Syms was feeling too wretched to call them to order.

"Oh, all right," she said wearily. Automatically her eyes

went to the clock on the blank wall facing her; the schoolroom had its front towards the sea. The same time again! It seemed to be a ritual with the Floyd girl. "But come back soon."

Well, thank heavens there was a half-hour break during which the children danced to tape-recorded music. She would have it earlier than usual today. Anyway, they would prefer it to the lesson. It was, she had for long suspected, the sole reason for their attendance.

She stored the music sheets away, closed the piano with a little bang and went a trifle unsteadily to the tape-recorder, which was on a table in the corner.

"You may have the recess now," she said. She plugged in the recorder and pressed down a switch.

There were excited cries of delight as young bodies in jeans and corduroys swayed and shuffled on the wooden floor.

"I'll be back," said Miss Syms. Nobody took any notice. She descended the flight of shallow steps to the ground floor, where she had her little office.

Outside, the sea raised its endless roar of defiance.

In between, on the dual rail tracks, two diesel trains passed, blaring at each other.

Overhead, the sun blazed down from a clear blue sky. It drenched everything with torrid heat. It shone impartially on life and death, on growth and decay.

Soon, in a few minutes, it would shine on the dead body of a girl.

Angela Floyd lay on a white rug on the sun-porch of the bungalow. In one hand she held a paper-back novel with a sexy cover. Within reach of her other hand was a long tumbler of orange juice in which floated cubes of ice. Nearby was a bottle of sunburn lotion.

Her eyes were not on the book but were staring into space. They were shaded by sunglasses. The sunglasses were all that she was wearing.

She put the book down and let the sun caress her body. Her face was oval and pretty. She was a brunette, with grey eyes,

A*

sensous lips and long, shapely legs. Her breasts were firm and round. She was just seventeen.

She reached out and took a few sips of the orange juice, resting on one elbow. As she felt the ice-cold liquid tingling down her throat she let her eyes linger on the bottle of lotion. Her lips drew back in a smile of anticipation. No need for her to apply the lotion herself. Soon there would be someone to do it for her.

She put the glass down and lay on her back again. She frowned slightly at the raucous chatter of the crows which flapped and pattered along the veranda rail. She hated the crows. They were everywhere—greedy, noisy, importunate. They would even come into the house given half a chance, ambling around like evil-looking little monks, snatching at everything and anything. They would steal the food from your plate, even from between your lips she sometimes thought. But now she felt too lazy to try to scare them away.

Eddie should be here by now. Wonderful Eddie, with the golden touch . . . It was nearly ten-thirty. The wrist-watch she had placed on the edge of the rug told her that.

Here he was at last! She felt a thrill run through her as she heard soft footsteps in the hall behind her. As on other days she closed her eyes, pretending to be asleep. Eddie would first put his hands over her eyes, then he would lean down and cover her with kisses.

Angela's body shook in anticipated ecstasy and her lips grew moist.

He was behind her now, bending over her.

Look out! It's not Eddie—

The warning blazed through her subconscious with the noise of a thousand sirens, jolting her eyes open.

It's not Eddie! It's someone holding an iron bar! They're going to kill me!

The sudden realisation seared her brain, but she was too terrified to move. She lay in a paralysis of fear. Her eyes were wide open in shocked disbelief and her mouth was uselessly agape.

She saw in a wordless horror the iron bar descend on her. It fell savagely, crushing her skull. It rose and fell over and over again until the soft, white, writhing body ceased to be soft and white any more.

And the white rug was no longer white.

From the giant mango trees in the school yard the whole stretch of the lane was visible.

It was visible only from a certain spot which had no obstructing foliage, and Judy Floyd had found it just over two weeks ago. The school had been started shortly after she had come with Mum and Dad two months ago on Dad's new assignment.

Judy had spent what were to her many happy hours on the tree. The other children avoided it because the mangoes on it were still too small and green and sour. It would take another month or so for them to ripen. Till then, Judy knew, she would have the tree to herself. It had given her something far more interesting than mangoes. It had given her moments of excitement and pleasure, and looked like continuing to do so.

There were only five houses in the lane between the main Colombo–Galle road and the sea. The house nearest the schoolroom did not count. It was old and high-roofed and the abode of Miss Syms and her sister. The other houses were of ultramodern design. Even Judy had been impressed by them.

What she did not know was that they had been built by one of those enterprising landowners who cater solely to topbracket-income Europeans and get fabulous rents in return for their investment.

What she did know was that Dad's firm had got the houses one jump ahead of some Embassy. The houses had everything, including air-conditioning. And they were only about two miles from Dad's office in the imposing new twenty-storey building in the Fort.

But these things did not interest Judy now. What interested her was that from her eyrie she could see right into the houses.

There hadn't been anything particularly interesting to see at the start.

On the left, near the top of the lane and on the same side as the schoolroom, was Robert Heston's house. Heston was Dad's boss. He was a flabby, near-bald Londoner with a paunch, whose shirts were always clinging clammily to his back, even with the air-conditioning on.

Some distance further down, on the opposite side, was Radley Allen's house, with its maze of aerials. Allen, like Heston, was a bachelor. He was plump and pink and very prim and proper—unlike Heston. Judy had quickly relegated Allen to the limbo she reserved for squares.

Facing Allen's house was that of the Millers—Mr and Mrs Conrad Miller and Eddie Vance, Mrs Miller's son by her first marriage. Judy's own house adjoined that of Allen's and facing it was the house in which lived Miss Syms and her sister.

For Judy the snag was that the only time she had a chance of surveying the scene was when there was practically no one in the houses. By ten o'clock Heston, Allen, the Millers and her parents had left. There remained only the Syms sisters—a couple of sour grapes, thought Judy—and Angela and Eddie. And a few stray cats and dogs. There were no servants. They had everything in the line of modern labour-saving devices.

There were some days when one or more of the others were at home, but even then it had been boring for Judy. Even the thrill of seeing the heat-sensitive Heston in the raw when he was alone had palled. And it wasn't much use knowing that Allen was a radio ham, that Miller seemed to prefer his whisky to his wife, and that Miss Syms's invalid sister spent most of her time in prayer and meditation.

Judy drew the line at spying on her parents, but not on her sister. She hated Angela, and Angela hated her. The sight of Angela sunbathing in the nude on the porch had, therefore, left her cold—until shortly after the arrival of Eddie.

That was barely two weeks ago, and from then on life had become very interesting for Judy. And for Angela, too, she reflected.

It was time now for the tryst. Around ten-thirty, when everybody else was away. That she had soon discovered, and that was why ten-thirty always found her out of the schoolroom. Never on a Sunday, of course, or what they called the Poya day that now passed for the Sunday holiday out here since last year.

She wished she could see more clearly. If she had a pair of binoculars, for instance—Dad had lost his when she most needed it. It had been exasperating. She would have to wait until he bought another pair. Then she could smuggle it out here for a clearer look. There was a big hollow near her perch where she could conceal it.

Judy settled herself more comfortably on the bough.

And so it was she saw the murder of her sister.

She watched it with the same sense of detachment with which she had watched television back in her former home at Croydon. But this she found far more thrilling.

It also gave her a shock.

For she saw the face of the killer. And it was the face of somebody she knew quite well.

CHAPTER II

Birds of Ill Omen

And whatever you do, omen or augury speak;
'tis a bird you are always repeating.
Benjamin Bickley Rogers: *The Birds*

"IT WAS DREADFUL," said Radley Allen. 'Horrible! I shall never forget it as long as I live."

He was seated in the lounge of the Floyds' house with a large brandy in his hand.

Facing him on a settee was Mrs Miller. Miller was mixing himself a drink at the miniature cocktail bar. Seated on an easy chair was Robert Heston.

From the adjoining room came the sounds of a woman weeping uncontrollably and the deep voice of a man mouthing words of comfort. Mary Floyd was taking the death of her daughter very hard.

They had all arrived a short while earlier. Allen had summoned them after calling the doctor and the police.

They hadn't let Mary Floyd go upstairs. They had told her that there had been an accident and that it would be wiser to wait until the doctor had attended on Angela.

But with swift feminine intuition she had divined that something was seriously wrong. She had insisted on going upstairs. And she had looked with a strange, dry-eyed intensity at the pitifully broken body on the floor. Then, like an automaton, she had walked back down the stairs, brushing aside their helping hands.

At the foot of the stairs she had collapsed. They had carried her into the study and laid her on a divan. Now at last the numbing horror had passed and she was crying.

They had left her there with her husband, white-faced and grim-eyed.

Upstairs, the police and the doctor were busy.

Allen passed an unsteady hand across his face. "It was the eye," he said. "The eye and those damned crows. It all began with the car giving trouble . . ."

He seemed to be speaking to himself, almost as though he were trying to commit every word to memory. He took another deep sip of the brandy and twin spots of colour appeared on his pale cheeks.

"The car wouldn't start," he said. "I tried everything I could think of . . . It had started all right first thing, but I got stuck near the gate. I saw you two passing—"

Mrs Miller nodded. She remembered, guiltily, that she had asked Conrad to stop and see what he could do to help Allen but Conrad, who was never in the best of moods in the mornings, had grunted surlily and driven on.

She hoped Allen had not noticed the sudden flush on her face.

Allen wiped his lips with a spotless white handkerchief.

"It was shortly after you left that I got the car started again. I left the engine running while I ran back, had a quick shower, put on a clean shirt and went out again. The engine had stopped once more."

He shuddered. "It was then I heard the crows. They're always noisy but this time they were noisier than ever. And I'd never seen so many all together. Something on the sun porch seemed to be attracting them. I knew that Jeff and Mary had gone to the office and I had heard Mary chasing Judy off to school. That left Angela alone in the house. I was wondering what could have happened when a couple of the crows flew over me, fighting over something. One of them broke away from the other and the . . . the thing they'd been quarrelling over dropped right at my feet. It was an eye—a human eye."

He looked as though he were about to be sick but gulped down another mouthful of brandy quickly and went on:

"For a minute I couldn't think straight. Then I began to run—towards the house. When I got to the porch I literally had to beat the crows off. She was lying there, blood everywhere. I managed to drag the rug into the house, with her still on it, then closed the french windows leading to the porch. There . . . there was nothing I could do for her. Whoever killed her must have been a maniac—"

Brandy slopped to the carpet as Allen raised the glass to his lips again. Eva Miller looked at him with something like admiration. For such a small, mild-mannered man he had done quite a lot; more than her boob of a husband would have done if he had been in the same situation. It just showed how deceptive appearances were.

Allen was a typical Briton, quiet and reserved but resourceful in an emergency. Conrad, on the other hand, had become an ugly American. He had spent most of his youth in America and had become thoroughly Americanised. He was bigly-made and loud-mouthed and floundering in a crisis. Apart from his superlative technical skill he was just a big soak. She took her eyes away from him as he came back with a refilled glass of whisky in a hairy hand and sat down beside her.

"You did very well, Mr Allen," she said. Her voice was soft and well modulated. She was a stout woman with enormous breasts. She was wearing a flowered print frock and flat-heeled shoes. "I am sure everyone appreciates—"

"Yeah, sure, honey," agreed Miller. He stole a swift glance at the silent Heston, took a noisy swig from his glass and smacked his lips appreciatively. "If you hadn't arrived when you did there'd have been nothing left of the poor gal. Those bloody crows can pick a carcase clean in ten minutes—"

"Conrad—please!" Eva Miller shuddered, though her eyes blazed angrily.

"Oh, all right, but you know what I mean." Miller set down his glass, reached into his trousers pocket for a packet of cigarettes. He held the packet out but the others refused. He lit up, let smoke trickle through his nostrils and said: "It was sure lucky Allen was there. It was a lucky break his car ran out on him."

Miller reached for his glass. His eyes were on Allen.

"Sure is funny, eh?"

"What do you mean by that?" Anger brought colour back into Allen's face. He half-rose from his chair. Miller waved him back with a placatory gesture.

"Relax, Rad. I was only—" He broke off as footsteps sounded on the stairs.

A short, sallow-faced man in a white drill suit was hurrying down, carrying a black bag in one hand.

"Well, doctor?" Heston looked up expectantly.

Dr Ralph Misso stopped at the foot of the stairs. He lived about a quarter of a mile away, on the main road, and was practically the family doctor.

"There's nothing I could have done for her, Mr Heston, even if she'd still been alive—which, thank God, she wasn't. She had been battered unmercifully. Fortunately for her, the first blow was fatal."

He bowed to Mrs Miller, nodded to the others. "I can't say how sorry I am. And now, will you please excuse me? I have another case on my hands."

He went across the lounge and knocked on the half-open door of the study.

In a silence broken only by the abandoned sobbing of Mary Floyd the white-sheeted remains of Angela had been borne on a stretcher into the waiting ambulance. The autopsy was to be held that afternoon.

The fingerprint men, the police photographer and Dr Misso had gone.

Upstairs, plain-clothes men were still busy. The little group in the hall could hear them moving about.

Mary Floyd was now seated on the settee. Floyd had one of his hands around her, drawing her to him. Despite her grief, Mary Floyd was a strikingly beautiful woman; a natural blonde, with a mass of hair making a halo around her face. She had a healthy skin, a well-moulded figure and eyes that normally were of a clear blue. Now they were red with weeping.

Jeffrey Floyd had an athletic build. His clean-shaven face, usually set in cheerful lines, was now drawn and haggard. With his free hand he was stroking his wife's hands as they lay on the lap of her blue and white two-piece suit.

"There, there, darling," he was saying ineffectually. His voice was harsh, unrecognisable. His jawbones stood out against his cheeks. "She's gone. There's only one thing we can do for her now—get the devil who killed her."

Mary Floyd broke into a fresh paroxysm of grief.

"Oh, my baby, my baby!" she wailed. "I shouldn't have left you alone. It was all my fault." She broke off suddenly and looked around her with dilated eyes. "Where's Judy?" She made as if to get up but Floyd pulled her gently back.

"It's all right, darling," he told her. "Judy's all right. She's still at school, you know."

"How do we know she's still there?" Mary Floyd's voice rose shrilly. "How do we know something hasn't happened to her as well? Oh, do something, will you! Find out if she's still there—"

Heston got to his feet. He was, as usual, perspiring freely, but of them all he was the coolest. He had to be, he kept telling himself. As chief representative of his firm in Ceylon, he was responsible for his staff. Besides, there was too much at stake.

"Don't worry, Mary. I'll check up."

He went to the phone set in an alcove and dialled the school. The voice of Emily Syms came over the wire.

"Oh, is that you, Mr Allen?" A flutter came into the voice. Emily had a soft spot for Allen. Such a nice man in her opinion, so quiet and unassuming. "Oh, I'm sorry. Mr Heston—your voice sounded similar. I must have been day-dreaming. The truth is, I'm having a terrible headache this morning. Terrible! And what with these children and the trouble they give—Oh, I'm sure they're very nice children, except one or two, of course, not that I'll ever mention names—and the noises of the sea and those awful diesel horns, they remind me of dis-embodied spirits wailing in the night, though in their case it's in the daytime as well . . . Oh dear, where was I? What's that? Judy Floyd? Yes, she's here. She was here all morning, from the time the music class began. Oh, not quite, I'm afraid—she went out about ten-thirty for, well—" Emily Syms hesitated and Heston could almost see her turning pink. "I don't know exactly when she came back. Do you want to speak to her? I could call her. It's no—"

"Oh no, it's all right, Emily," Heston broke in hurriedly. "Will you hold on, please?" He covered the mouthpiece with one hand and looked at Floyd. "Judy's at school, quite safe. What do you want me to tell Miss Syms?"

Floyd held a hurried consultation with his wife, went across and took the receiver from Heston.

'Miss Syms? Floyd here, Judy's father. Now listen carefully, please. There has been an accident here. It would be better if Judy did not come home to lunch today. Tell her to go with the Gregg children when their car comes for them. Tell her I'll fix things up with Mr Gregg. Got that? Thank you."

He hung up before Emily Syms could put the questions that were crowding on her lips.

CHAPTER III

Blue Skies Blues

I'm thinking, Pierre, how that damned strange quality
Called honesty got a footing in the world.
Thomas Otway: *Venice Preserved*

FREDDIE DE SOYSA almost drooled.

Freddie was one of the parasites of Colombo. He was a young man who lived on his wits and on women.

Many years ago Freddie de Soysa had found that he had a certain fascination for women, and he had lost no time in making the best of it—for himself.

He was a lean, swarthily handsome Sinhalese, with flashing white teeth, a thin wisp of a moustache and a mass of black hair slicked straight with the liberal application of a mixture of brilliantine and coconut oil. He always contrived to be well-dressed. It was an essential part of his stock-in-trade.

He came from a good family and had had an expensive education in one of the leading public schools in Colombo. He had also acquired expensive tastes at an early age.

The truth was, he had found, he couldn't indulge in his varied pursuits without money. Especially as each one of his pursuits was a woman. He had got over that difficulty by forging cheques belonging to the firm of tea brokers where he had been employed. He had got along very well until he had been found out.

Family influence had saved him from prosecution. But it had meant the loss of his job and the complete and irrevocable severance of all family ties.

From that time Freddie de Soysa had drifted along on his own. With his education, his air of breeding and his natural talent for dishonesty he had got along tolerably well. He found that he need not have to work for a living. Not while there were suckers around.

Women were his especial prey. In Freddie's eyes they were natural born suckers. They were waiting to be sucked dry—by someone who knew the technique. And Freddie took pride in the belief that he knew the technique backwards. He became an expert in the art of ensnaring women and relieving them of their surplus cash.

Freddie had found out that some of the most fruitful hunting-grounds were the big hotels in Colombo. There he could almost unfailingly come across a woman just ripe for plucking.

He had arrived at the Walton shortly before four in the evening. He was nattily dressed, as ever, in a blue lounge suit, white shirt, light grey tie, grey socks with a thin red stripe and gleaming black shoes.

The lounge was half-full when he sat at a table and ordered a pint of the beer brewed locally in the hill resort of Nuwara Eliya.

He lifted the mug to his lips and let his practised eyes rove over the tables.

Nothing much, he told himself disappointedly. The usual crowd of local folk, a sprinkling of obvious and uninteresting-looking tourists and—

Freddie de Soysa's heart gave a sudden leap.

There, in a far corner, almost hidden by a noisy family, was a girl whose appearance literally took his breath away.

He cursed the noisy family, quietly eased his chair back and looked at her. And what he saw caused him to pass his tongue delicately over his lips.

She had a beautiful face, with high cheekbones and a firmly moulded chin, honey-blonde hair, and a shapely figure with softly rounded curves. Her long legs were crossed, exposing a portion of moulded nyloned thigh. She looked poised and elegant, simply but expensively dressed and the fact that she was alone provided a combination which Freddie found irresistible.

This, he thought exultantly, is my lucky day.

He rose, carrying his half-empty mug, and made his way to the corner table where she sat. "Do you mind?" he asked, indicating one of the chairs.

She gave him a swift, abstracted smile which encouraged Freddie still further. "Not at all," she said. Her voice was soft but rich in texture—like silk, thought Freddie.

He sat on her left, against the wall, resisting the impulse to brush his knees against her as he passed. This one looked as though she might play hard to get; some of them did—at first. At close quarters she was almost more devastating than at a distance. And Freddie was a connoisseur.

He moistened his lips and tried to keep his voice steady. "Forgive me," he said, and for a moment he had a panicky impression that someone else was speaking through his mouth. "Forgive me, but can I get you something to drink?"

She indicated the glass at her side, which was half-full. "Thank you, but no. I have something."

"Champagne, perhaps? Or would you care to try something very special. Something local? When in Rome, you know—"

He flashed a smile at her and before she could reply he beckoned a hovering waiter.

"Two full white arracks on the rocks," he told the white-coated, white-saronged figure. He leaned back in his chair and smiled again. "I'm sure you'll like it. It's our national drink, distilled from coconut toddy. There are several varieties and the best is as good as whisky. Allow me to introduce myself—"

She was looking directly into his face now; her eyes were deep blue, fringed by long dark lashes. Freddie almost swooned. Recovering himself he said: "My name is Frederick de Silva—my friends call me Freddie. I'm a tea-planter from up-country, on a short trip to Colombo."

"My name is Dane. Paula Dane. I'm a private secretary."

"Your boss is a very lucky man, Miss Dane, if I may say so." Freddie smirked. "May I know if he is also in the tea business."

"No." The word was clipped. Freddie waited expectantly

but she did not offer any further information.

"But he *is* in business?" he persisted.

"Really, Mr de Silva, I cannot discuss my employer's affairs with a stranger—"

"Of course not. I'm sorry." Freddie smiled at her. A very private and confidential secretary, eh? Well, so much the better. The more private and confidential they were the better he liked them.

The waiter had arrived with the drinks. Freddie handed her one of the glasses and raised his own glass. She grimaced at the first sip of the amber-coloured liquid, which looked like whisky but was even more potent. Freddie gave her an encouraging grin.

"Go on. It's the best stuff. You'll be asking for more."

He must feed this line out carefully, he told himself. She was a fish worth catching. As she sipped he went on, expansively:

"There's lovely sea bathing down at Mount Lavinia. It's just a few miles from here. Would you like me to take you?" He added: "I'm afraid my car is under repair at the moment, but we could have a taxi—"

She put down the glass and he noticed, with disappointment, that it was still three-quarters full.

"I'm so sorry," she said. "You must excuse me. I have some work to do."

"Another time then, perhaps?" In his eagerness Freddie leaned forward over the table, reaching out his hand towards her. She made a gesture as though in response, but her hand knocked against the glass and the contents splashed across the table on to Freddie's immaculately pressed trousers. He sprang upright, choking back a curse.

"Oh dear, how very clumsy of me!" she said contritely. "Now you'll have to go and change—"

"It's quite all right." Freddie tried to sound off-hand. "It'll soon dry in the sun." His expression changed as Paula also got to her feet, picking up her handbag at the same time. "You're not going?" he demanded.

"I'm afraid so. I have work to do—"

"Oh, but I was hoping to get to know you better, Miss Dane —much better! And I was hoping you would like to get to know me."

She was walking out of the lounge, moving gracefully, her blonde head turning neither to right nor left. Freddie pattered after her, carefully shielding his damp trousers from the vulgar gaze by keeping between Paula and the wall. The lifts to the twenty floors were on the right, at the end of a long corridor lined with glittering shops. The corridor ended at the hotel's swimming pool.

Paula walked down the shallow steps to the edge of the pool and stood staring down reflectively into the water. Freddie was right beside her.

At least, one moment he was beside her. Then Paula stepped back suddenly, seeming to stumble, and the next moment he found himself in the water, swallowing a great deal of it while he spluttered in mingled astonishment and rage.

"Oh dear!" said Paula again, wringing her hands as she stood looking down at his splashing form. "I don't know what has got into me today. I'm so clumsy. First the drink and now this—you *can* swim, can't you, Mr da Silva?"

But Freddie was already clambering out of the pool, as wet as a drowned rat, his hair looking as though glued to his head, his ears burning with the sound of laughter from the spectators who had witnessed his discomfiture.

"I really am very sorry," said Paula. She gave him a flashing smile, then turned and walked away. Freddie looked after her and his expression was no longer admiring.

"All right, my girl," he muttered as he leaked his way back across the lounge to summon a taxi. "I'll get even for this, you see if I don't."

Freddie de Soysa was no believer in the turned-cheek and the love-thy-enemy axiom.

Gemini Herat, Inspector-General of the Ceylon Police, leaned back in his chair and smiled across the paper-strewn desk at his visitor.

"Well, Mr Blake, it looks as though we've got this gang of dope-peddlers tied up at last—thanks to you."

Sexton Blake held up a protesting hand. "I'm afraid I didn't do anything much," he said. "I wouldn't have made much headway but for the help I received from you and your men. I got off to a good start here. It's not often that I come across such splendid co-operation. That's one point I'll not fail to mention in my report to Interpol!"

Blake and Paula had arrived that afternoon by Indian Airlines Viscount from Bombay. They had landed at Ratmalana Airport, the small airfield on the southern outskirts of Colombo, and driven from there to the capital in a car provided by Herat.

It had been the end of an arduous chase that had brought them from London to Colombo and its smugglers' paradise at Uswetakeiyawa, then on to Bangkok and its torrid night clubs, from Don Muang Airport to the fleshpots of Singapore and back through Bangkok to the teeming slums of Calcutta.

Blake hadn't even had the time to visit the grave of his brother, Nigel.* He was after an international dope gang and the trail finally led from Calcutta to Bombay and then back to Colombo. Now, to quote Paula, he had all the "dope" on the gang. Under the arrangements with Interpol the police would do the mopping-up. He knew he could count on Herat to do that. He was also making use of the opportunity to renew an old friendship.

The two men were seated in Herat's sanctum in Police Headquarters. It was a large, airy room with walls of light green distemper on which were hung framed portraits of past Inspectors-General of Police and the various Prime Ministers. The room was solid and old-fashioned, for the sprawling building near the harbour dated back to Dutch times, when the buildings that formed the Fort were designed to withstand sieges.

On Blake's right was an oblong conference table with high-

---

*For the story of Nigel Blake see *Fire Over India* by W. Howard Baker.

backed chairs ranged around it. Through the windows behind Herat and between the intervening buildings of the Customs and the old passenger jetty, Blake could see a section of the harbour with some cargo ships at anchor and motor launches darting about like fish in a pond.

Herat sighed. "The world would be a better place if there were more co-operation. Professional envy and jealousy can be terrible things! Anyway, as I was saying, thanks to you I can tell my men when and where they can grab the gang. They won't get away, I promise you—"

He broke off as one of the phones on his desk rang. With a muttered apology he lifted the receiver. "Herat here."

He listened for a moment, then his face lit up. "Oh, good, Van! Thank you for calling. I particularly wanted to see you as soon as you came back. Will you please come up here with the file on the Floyd girl?"

Herat replaced the handset and turned to Blake. He was looking very grave.

"I've got something that may interest you, Mr Blake. In fact, I'm sure it will. Excuse me again." He picked up another phone and gave an order: "I'm not to be disturbed for the next hour—on no account."

"As big as that?" asked Blake.

"Bigger," said Herat sombrely. His eyes flashed an unspoken appeal. He was a soldierly looking man with a deeply lined but pleasant face. A first-class administrator, he had served in various capacities in the Civil Service before his appointment to his present post. A hard but just task-master, ruthless when necessary, he had set out first to rid the Force of corruption by improving conditions of service and also to rid it of political interference. It wasn't an easy job. It was a thankless one, and he had made many powerful enemies. But Herat wouldn't give up. He was still trying.

Sexton Blake knew of the struggle Herat had been going through. Herat could always count on his support in his war on big crime and bigger chicanery. He could see how the struggle had taken its toll of the man, in his care-worn face and the

26

premature greying of his hair. Herat had aged a lot since they had last met.

Blake offered his cigarette case and they lit up.

Herat pushed an ashtray across to him. "I'm afraid I'm taking a bit of a liberty with you, Mr Blake. In the circumstances, however, I feel it is justified. You see, I know something of your interest in the unusual and I shall be glad to have your views on something which has been baffling us. I've put my best man on the job—Detective Chief Inspector Vandebona—but even he hasn't been able to make any headway. I have asked him to bring the connected dossier so that we may have the benefit of your expert advice."

Blake smiled. "But of course," he said.

CHAPTER IV

Kiss and Kill?

No, like a bank for love to lie and play on;
Not like a corse; or if, not to be buried,
But quick and in mine arms.
            Shakespeare: *The Winter's Tale*

'WELL, MR BLAKE, that's the lot. What do you make of it?"

It was an hour later. Blake and the police chief had heard out in silence the detailed account by Detective Chief Inspector Vandebona of the investigations into the murder of Angela Floyd.

Sexton Blake did not reply at once. He was deep in thought. He had been shown the police photographs of the murdered girl and he was thinking how much he would like to bring to book the perpetrator of such a ghastly crime.

"At first", went on Herat, "we thought it was an open-and shut case. Nothing more than a *crime passionel*, in fact, particularly as the young man concerned—Eddie Vance—was missing at the time. He is still missing, for a matter of fact, despite the all-stations call I have sent out for him."

The thin, gangling man seated beside Blake riffled through the pages of the dossier. He was dark-visaged, with thinning black hair and a diffident manner. Detective Chief Inspector Hubert Vandebona, better known in the Police Department and the underworld as "Bones", also had brains, which was why he had been detailed for this case. Blake had taken an instant liking to him and he knew that the regard was mutual.

"I suppose", he said, "every one of the statements had been checked?"

"All but two," said Vandebona. "One is Heston's. I'm afraid it'll take some time. The other is Miller's."

Blake nodded. "Unfortunately, these statements appear to lead nowhere. We must, of course, not overlook the possibility that some outsider is the killer. Any moron who knew that the girl was alone could have walked in—"

Herat frowned. "Yes, it's not going to be easy." He was very glad of Blake's presence. The trouble was he could not call Blake in on the case officially; but he knew he would give him all the help he could unofficially. In any case, Blake was due to return to England in a couple of days.

England had all the luck, Herat reflected sourly. He was thinking of Ceylon's phenomenal record of an average of two reported murders a day and of the recent wave of big crime. In the past, homicides had been easy to tackle. But things were different now. Cold-blooded, planned murder was taking the place of the sudden, spur-of-the-moment killings. There were gang feuds, hired killers and hand-bomb throwers. The official murder score for last year had been six hundred and eighty— an all-time record. If only there were someone like Sexton Blake here!

Blake was saying slowly: "The only evidence against young Eddie Vance, your first suspect, is that he is missing since last night. But apart from his stepfather, there is no one to confirm exactly when he left the house. Even if he left last night he still had ample time to return this morning, commit the crime, and vanish.

"Then there is Miller. According to their statements, Mr and Mrs Miller and Mr and Mrs Floyd can account for their movements at the office after they left home between nine and nine-thirty." Blake was reading from notes he had scribbled. "According to the medical evidence, the girl was murdered at ten-thirty. Miller says he left the office about ten to cash a cheque at his bank in Prince Street, a short distance away."

Vandebona broke in: "We have verified from Mr and Mrs Floyd that he left the office at 10.02 a.m. but there is no trace of any transaction by him at the bank."

"And what", asked Blake, "has he to say to that?"

29

Vandebona was apologetic. "I have not been able to question him again yet. The check-up at the bank was made while I was at the inquest this afternoon. In fact, I received the information just before I came up here."

"You'd better question him again, of course," said Herat. "But I don't see how he could have committed the murder. Remember, Allen was near his gate tinkering with his car. He could have seen Miller coming back."

"It might just be possible, sir. He wouldn't have driven back in his car. He would have taken a taxi to near the top of the lane—it's called Kumudu Mawata, which means Lotus Lane— and walked down. Allen would have been too busy to notice. It's rather far-fetched, I know, but I'm having a check made on taxi drivers who dropped fares in the vicinity of Kumudu Mawata between 10.05 and 10.30 a.m."

Blake gave an appreciative smile. "Bones" certainly was painstaking.

"All right," he said, looking up from his notes again. "So much for Miller, for the moment. Now, there's Allen. He was the only person near the scene at the time of the crime. Apart from the Syms sisters, of course."

Blake stubbed his cigarette in an ashtray. "The only persons who, apparently, could not have been anywhere near the scene were Heston, the Floyds and Mrs Miller. Allen was the nearest. According to his statement he was held up because his car was giving trouble."

He looked inquiringly at Vandebona.

"I checked up on the car, sir. I thought it queer that the car —it's a new Anglia—should give starting trouble. There was nothing wrong with it. Nothing at all."

Vandebona paused to let the words sink in. "All that was wrong had nothing to do with the mechanism. The petrol tank was empty. It was bone dry."

Herat flicked ash off his cigarette. "Oh, come now, Van! The fact that Allen's petrol tank was empty doesn't mean that he is guilty of murder, surely?"

"Let's suppose he is, sir. He would then need some excuse to be there when the others had left, wouldn't he? When I questioned him about it he said he knew there wasn't much petrol left in the tank but that he wasn't worried because he would have filled up on the way to the office in the morning. There's a filling station a short distance from the turn-off."

"So he faked the breakdown?"

"I'm assuming it, sir." Vandebona glanced at Blake, who gave him an encouraging nod. "He didn't want to meddle with the engine, so he drained off the petrol. He must have returned home last night practically without petrol for that very purpose."

"But it was Allen who found the body," persisted Herat.

"Of course. It doesn't prove he didn't commit the crime. He had the time and the opportunity. Also, his clothes were blood-stained—though he explains those away by stating that he got them when he dragged the girl—still on the rug—off the sun-porch."

"That's logical," nodded Herat. "There was blood everywhere. I've never seen such a mess."

Blake put a question. "What other reason have you for assuming Allen might be the killer?"

"This, sir. Allen is a bachelor. By all accounts a perfectly respectable bachelor—but even perfectly respectable bachelors, like perfectly respectable married men—have had their heads turned by a pretty face. What I'm saying now is pure conjecture, of course, but it could have been that Allen staged the car breakdown and waited until the Millers had gone. He knew that the younger girl, Judy was at school. and that Angela was alone in the house; perhaps he also knew that she was in the habit of sun-bathing, nude, on the porch outside her bedroom. So he went into the house and tried to make advances to her. She repelled him, and in a frenzy of anger he struck her down—"

"One thing," said Blake quickly. "The murder weapon. What was it, and has it been found?"

"No, sir. The medical evidence indicates that it was exceptionally heavy—an iron bar, perhaps."

"And was there such an iron bar in the Floyd's house?"

"The Floyds say no, sir. None that they knew of."

"It is highly unlikely that the dead girl would have kept an iron bar in her bedroom—or on the sun-porch?"

Vandebona looked a little puzzled. "I should hardly think so—"

"In that case, the murderer could have brought it with him," remarked Blake. "Indicating that the killing was premeditated. It seems highly improbable that Allen would have gone to pay court to Angela Floyd armed with an iron bar."

Vandebona nodded. "It's a good point, sir. Nevertheless, assuming that Allen was the murderer—by this time his clothes would be badly stained with blood. Short of getting back unobserved to his own house and destroying them—always a risky procedure and certain to bring the gravest suspicion on him if he failed—the only thing he could do was to raise the alarm himself. Thus the bloodstains would be explained—and he *had* to find a way to explain them. The crows helped. The noise they would have made would have attracted anyone's attention, even those who are used to seeing and hearing the birds. Anything dead, sir—" He broke off apologetically.

Blake smiled. "You've made out quite a case against him, haven't you? But have you the evidence to back it?"

"No, sir. Everything ties in with his story. The murder weapon is the real clue, and that's still missing."

"You've searched the house and grounds?"

"Thoroughly. If Allen never left the premises after finding the body—his story—then the weapon must be hidden somewhere around. Buried, perhaps. I've got men still looking for it."

"What about this boy, Eddie Vance?" asked Blake. "You say they were friends?"

"Some say more than friends. But it seems hard to believe that a boy like Eddie could have made such a savage attack on Angela. Remember, whoever killed her went on hitting her long after she was dead . . . It's more feasible that she repulsed Allen rather than young Miller.''

Vandebona spread out his bony hands, looking at Blake. "Allen had both the time and the opportunity to kill the girl—and the motive," he said.

"What about the Syms sisters?" asked Blake. "You say Miss Emily was at the school; but what about Bella, the eldest one? Isn't she an invalid? Did she see—or hear—anything?"

"She says no," the inspector replied with his customary caution. "She says she saw nothing—and heard nothing, either. The latter could be true; you see, she's deaf.''

"But she was there, at home. Could she have had any reason for wanting to kill Angela?''

"None that I can see. She's a bit of a religious maniac. Spends most of the time praying.''

"But she can move around? What I mean is, she's not a cripple, in a wheelchair?'' asked Blake.

"No, sir. But she hardly ever ventures out of the house; Miss Emily does most of the shopping. Come to that, Miss Emily has nobody to confirm her statement that she was in her office, resting because of a headache. None of the boys or girls was out at the time of the murder, except the dead girl's sister. I questioned her and she said she went to the lavatory and saw and heard nothing suspicious.'' For some reason Vandebona did not seem inclined to discuss Judy Floyd further.

He went on: "There's also Heston. He's the chief representative of the big firm that is doing the work on this new power scheme. He didn't go to the office in the morning—not straight away. He says he left for Galle on business. That's seventy-two miles from here, down south—'' The inspector looked at Blake as he explained. "He says he left home about nine, but that on the way he remembered that some important papers he required were in the office, so he turned back. Reached the office shortly before the message came from Allen about the murder. He immediately went over with the Floyds and the Millers.''

"Heston says he doesn't know exactly where he turned back, but I'm having his story checked. He could have had time to commit the murder. As for motive, and the rest of it, he could have had the same motive as Allen. Angela Floyd was an extremely attractive girl—and knew how to make the most of it."

Blake settled himself back in his chair. "You've presented the whole thing admirably," he told Vandebona. In his eyes was a far-away look which Tinker, Paula, Marion Lang or Miss Louise Pringle would have instantly recognised. He added on a wistful note: "It certainly is an intriguing problem. But I don't think I can offer you much in the way of advice at the moment. The case appears to be in good hands."

He glanced at Herat. "Of course, the sooner you find young Eddie Vance the better. Heston and Allen should bear watching. Then there are the two Syms sisters—one of them with a headache, the other with time on her hands; it's remarkable what middle-aged spinsters with time on their hands can do. I hope you'll let me know the result of your inquiries about Heston. I have an idea that I know him."

He got to his feet. "The most important thing is to find the murder weapon. By that we may succeed in tracing the murderer. On the face of it, it would appear that Allen is your chief suspect, but I won't commit myself on that score. Now I'm afraid I must be going. You can get in touch with me at the hotel. Today's Saturday; I'll be there until Monday night. Then I'll be leaving by plane for England." He held out his hand to Herat. "It's been a pleasure meeting you again."

"That makes two of us," said Herat.

They shook hands and Blake turned to Vandebona.

"I hope you won't be needing me again. But if you do, I'll be glad to give what help I can—time permitting. Good-bye—and good luck."

Sexton Blake paid off the taxi, added a generous tip and walked up the polished steps into the marble-and-bronze foyer of the hotel. He glanced into the crowded lounge on his left, expecting to see Paula there, but there was no sign of her. Then his ears caught one or two snippets of conversation which caused him to pause, lift his eyebrows quizzically, then give a faint smile.

He went to the lift and arrived at his suite on the tenth floor. He knocked on the door of Paula's room.

"Is that you, chief?" came Paula's voice. "Come in."

Blake stepped into the sitting room. His secretary, cool and composed, was seated in a comfortable-looking armchair, polishing her fingernails. She looked up at him and smiled.

"Had a good day, chief?" she asked.

"An interesting one," replied Blake. "What about you? You've not been too bored, I hope." He added: "What's this I hear about an accident in the swimming-pool? A man fell into the water—"

"Did he tumble or was he pushed?" asked Paula demurely.

Blake laughed. "I gathered you were involved. The description of the young woman was very flattering. Who was the importunate—and unfortunate—young man?"

Paula gave a delicate shiver. "He told me his name was Frederick da Silva, and that he was a tea-planter. He was obviously lying. He looked like a cab-driver to me—no reflection on cab-drivers, of course. He tried to get fresh and I—er—discouraged him." She added: "He really was a very unpleasant person."

Blake stooped to pour himself a cup of coffee from the still steaming coffee-pot on the table at Paula's side.

"Perhaps it's just as well we're leaving here on Monday," he remarked. "In Colombo, unpleasant young men can sometimes be very unpleasant indeed."

CHAPTER V

Wake up Screaming

Heav'n from all creatures the book of Fate
All but the page inscribed, their present state.
Pope: *Essays on Man*

"BUD," protested Freddie de Soysa, "I godda code."

"So what?" asked the voice within him inexorably. "A little thing like that shouldn't stand in your way. Be a man!"

Freddie let the insult pass by. He had a good excuse, he comforted himself; he was feeling as weak as a kitten and as lousy as a louse.

"A—ah—ahtishoo-oo!" exploded Freddie. He blew his nose vigorously into an unclean handkerchief. "See what I mean?"

"All it means", pursued the hateful voice, "is that you are setting up a defence mechanism against doing something you haven't the guts to do. You are trying to make your present condition an excuse for not getting even with the woman who is the direct cause of it."

"Bud whad cad I do?" sniffed Freddie. "She's no ordinary woman, and you know id. Di'n'd you hear the hotel manager say, while I was waiting for a taxi, thad she's the privade secretary of Sexton Blake? Thad's the world's mos' famous dedecdive, in case you don'd know id."

"I know it, idiot, that's just the point!" snapped the voice impatiently. "You're letting yourself be scared by Blake's reputation. He's just a human being, isn't he? Now, what I'm trying to get into your thick head is that because it's Blake you should take a greater interest in the matter. This may be the turning point of your life. How long do you want to continue this hand-to-mouth existence? Can't you see a good thing when it's placed right under your nose? You'd better wipe it again, by the way. Can't you realise that this chance, if handled right, may raise you to dizzy heights?"

"Id's already pud me in code wader," mumbled Freddie. "I don' wanna ged indo hod wader."

"Hah! You're killing me! If you've finished being funny, listen to me, you dope. Blake can't be here for his health. If he was, he wouldn't be staying in Colombo—he'd have gone to a place like Nuwara Eliya up in the hills, where the climate'll remind him of England. He must be here on business, and whatever business Blake is on is always big. Find out what that business is."

"Whad for? Id's her I wanna get even with."

"What for? Have I got to draw a map for you? Don't you realise that where there is big crime there are big pickings? Don't you see that here's a first-class chance for you to help yourself?"

"You think so?" Despite himself. Freddie was becoming interested.

"If I didn't I wouldn't be telling you all this."

"But whaddo I do?"

"That's up to you," said the voice wearily. "Find out what Blake is here for. Keep your eyes and ears open—not your nose and mouth."

"All ride," said Freddie. "I'll do id. But nod tonide. Led me sleep now."

Judy had been packed off to bed early. But she wasn't sleeping.

It wasn't because she was in a strange house. Allen had offered them the run of his house when Mum had refused to sleep at home that night. Judy wasn't sleeping because her mind was too busy.

She was glad she didn't have to come home that afternoon.

It would have been a bit too soon. She might have given away her secret by some incautious word or gesture.

But now she was fully prepared to play her self-appointed role—until as long as it suited her.

She thought with relish of the uncomfortable time she had given the tall, bony inspector who had questioned her. "Where did you go", he had asked her, "when you left the music class at ten-twenty-five?" And she promptly responded "To the loo" and started to give him details. He had quickly stopped her. He wouldn't come back to question her again in a hurry!

In her he had met his Waterloo. That was rich. She felt pleased with herself at the play on words. It was something with which she could cap her story to a wide-eyed, admiring group of friends.

At first she had resented being sent with the Gregg children. They were a stuffy pair. The boy, David, was only thirteen but he was always with his books or stuck away in his "den" at home with its horrid chemical smells and its jumble of lathes and tools. His ten-year-old sister, Alice, was an equal loss with her eternal party manners and her baby-doll face. Judy believed she even washed behind her ears without being told.

But Judy had made good use of the few hours she had spent at their home in the exclusive, tree-lined Buller's Road near what was formerly the Colombo Racecourse. Now the grandstand and main enclosures accommodated the overflow of thousands of students from the University of Ceylon at Peradeniya on the outskirts of the hill capital, Kandy. And on the green turf where horses had thundered were the permanent structures of the vote-catching Industrial Exhibition held a few months before the general election of March 1960, and which were now the venue of the Jatika Pola or National Fair held on Poya days, at which housewives had the opportunity of buying vegetables and other home needs much cheaper than in the black market and at which black marketeers made larger purchases to fill their counters.

These details had been given to her by the lisping Alice, who seemed to have an encyclopedic knowledge of such matters.

Alice, in fact, considered herself an authority on local politics and history and had been eager to air all of that knowledge. Judy had listened as patiently as she could. All the while she had been gloating inwardly. What was Alice's store of knowledge compared with the knowledge she had acquired that morning—knowledge which she shared with a killer?

She had got rid of Alice with the least possible delay and had spent most of her time after lunch in David's "den", finding that the way to his heart was through his smelly, messy hobbies. David had responded enthusiastically to the show of interest, with the result that she had picked up many things which she felt would come in handy. She had picked them up in more ways than one.

Judy stirred restlessly in her bed in the room adjoining that in which her parents were sleeping. Across the corridor she could hear Allen snoring in the guest room into which he had shifted.

She tiptoed to the door and bolted it.

Emily Syms, too, was not sleeping.

For one thing the sound of the rats scampering about in the attic worried her, for she had a horror of rats. Bella, of course, was different. Rats did not scare Bella.

But what really kept her awake were the thoughts that kept crowding into her mind regarding the death of Angela Floyd. It had been a horrible death. Death, of course, was always unpleasant, but the manner of Angela's death had been particularly dreadful.

And to think that she had died practically in sin! Emily Syms did her utmost never to think evil of others, especially of the dead. Still, there were certain limits to human decency and behaviour. It was as if a justly angered Providence had struck Angela down.

At least, so Bella had said, and Emily was inclined to agree with her. Bella, naturally, would think in no other way. Her feet had always been firmly planted on the path of righteousness. Angela's death, and the circumstances in which she met her death, with its overtones of sex and lust, should be a warning to modern youth and their way of life, she had said. Nevertheless, she would pray for Angela.

Dear Bella, thought Emily. Always so full of rectitude. If only she hadn't been condemned to the life of an invalid, what a force she might have been in the world! She might have been a great reformer, with her ardour, her single-mindedness.

But there, that was the hand of Providence again. Providence had decreed that Bella Syms should be lost to the world and that she, Emily, should sacrifice everything in life to attend to her sister's needs.

There was nothing she should not be able, and glad, to do for dear Bella.

Hadn't she done something for her that day?

Or had she?

Emily Syms felt confused. Her head still ached. With a sigh she turned towards the wall, away from the night-light. She must sleep.

She felt herself being drawn along a giant funicular railway that stretched right out to the sky.

In the adjoining room Bella Syms lay on her back in the dark, saying her prayers.

Whereas Emily was thin and austere-looking, Bella was big and raw-boned. She had once been plump, but now the flesh sagged on her like the wrinkles in a half-collapsed tent. But her face was still round and smooth, her lips firm and her eyes bright.

It was Emily who would have filled the role of an invalid to a nicety, but Providence—as Emily would have been the first to point out—moved in mysterious ways.

It was Emily whom Bella was thinking about now. There had been something different about Emily today. True, she had pleaded a headache, which was understandable, but Bella felt there was something else.

Something which Emily was trying to hide from her.

She knew every nuance of Emily's needs and could read her

like an open book, so she knew she couldn't be wrong. And for Emily to keep something from her was unthinkable. Emily had never before kept anything from her.

There had been a subtle change in her, particularly after the inspector had left. The inspector had questioned each of them separately, so she couldn't know exactly what Emily had said. Or not said.

The inspector—she couldn't recollect the name but it seemed to suit his appearance—had been very nice and polite. He had asked her what she had been doing that morning. Had she had any occasion to leave the house? Had she heard or seen anything untoward?

She had answered to the best of her ability, twiddling the little knob on the battery of the earpiece she carried in the pocket of her dress. Sometimes, she explained, when the battery was low, it was difficult to hear properly.

She was wondering what Emily had said, for the change in her had come after she had been talking to the inspector.

Well, she would find out eventually. Emily sometimes got so confused. She would look into it tomorrow.

Bella Syms yawned. She was feeling sleepy. She hurried through her prayers, then mouthed the final prayer—one that she never failed to recite every night:

'. . . *and preserve us, O Lord, from the enemy.*'

It was a prayer she had unfailingly said since September 3rd, 1939, the day World War II began.

For Bella Syms the war had not ended yet.

B*

CHAPTER VI

Two for the Road

Sir Wilful is set in to drinking, madam,
in the parlour.
Congreve: *The Way of the World*

DETECTIVE Chief Inspector Vandebona knew he had a busy
night ahead of him. Recording the statements and having
them checked up, wherever possible, had taken quite a lot of
time. Then there had been the inquest proceedings. They had
been purely formal, but the autopsy and the recording of the
medical and police evidence and that of Allen, who had found
the body, had gone on till well in the evening.

The Judicial Medical Officer had testified that Angela Floyd
had died of injuries caused by a brutal attack on her with a
blunt instrument. There were multiple injuries, each of which
he had described in dispassionate detail.

The first blow, on the head, had caused death instantane-
ously. But the killer had gone on hitting his victim, on head,
face and body. He did not rule out the possibility of a homicidal maniac. The girl was not a virgin, nor had she been
pregnant. There had been no sexual assault. Some paranoics,
however, would derive sexual satisfaction from the mere act of
battering the nude body.

The murder weapon had not been found, and the police
were still searching for it.

After the evidence of identification by an ashen-faced Allen
and the police evidence, which disclosed nothing of any

significance, the coroner had recorded a verdict of homicide by some person or persons unknown, and had adjourned the inquest for a week pending further police inquiries.

All this had taken time. Now more time would have to be spent on completing the checks on the statements.

Already one lie had been exposed. Miller's story of a trip to the bank was proved to be false. Vandebona reflected grimly that he would have to find out the truth behind that. He would tackle Conrad Miller before doing anything else. Maybe Miller would change his ground when he realised that he had landed himself in a mess. His wife had seemed to be a sensible woman.

As Sexton Blake had suggested, he would be wise to do some very definite checking-up on Heston. The chief representative of World Power Ltd, would have to substantiate his story of the forgotten papers.

Vandebona had reached the door of his office. He would have to clear up some minor routine matters before going out. As he entered the room the telephone on the desk rang. His assistant, a sergeant, who was busy writing at a smaller table, rose, but Vandebona waved him back. He hurried across and picked up the receiver.

"Oh, is that you, Inspector?"

For a moment he could not place the soft voice.

"Mrs Miller speaking. It's about that bank business—my husband, I mean. I think he's been rather foolish. I've questioned him and he told me he did not go to the bank from the office this morning, although he told you he did. The fact is, he dropped in at a bar and had some drinks. You know how it is. Especially with him."

"Does he know the name of the place?"

"That's just it, Inspector. He says he can't remember. He says that if he'd known in advance that he was to be involved in a murder inquiry, he'd have made a note of it. All he knows is that it's one of those small places in the Fort. He's been there before but he can't remember the name—one of these local names he finds unpronounceable. Besides, all he's concerned about is the drink, he says, not the name of the bar."

43

Vandebona smiled. "Look, Mrs Miller, it would be better if I could question your husband personally. Do you mind if I call now—if he's in?"

"Not at all, Inspector." There was a cordial note in the soft voice. "You're welcome any time. Conrad is in, and I'll keep him here until you come."

Vandebona gladly handed over the remaining paper-work on his desk to the sergeant.

"This should keep you happy, Silva," he said, ignoring the other's martyred look. "Have a good time!"

He decided against taking a police car. The distance was short, so he went to the bus halt near Police Headquarters and bought himself a ten-cents ticket on a double-decker bound to the Dehiwela Zoo.

He got off at the Kollupitiya junction, crossed the road and walked down the lane, with which he had become familiar now.

Mrs Miller admitted him into the house. She was wearing grey, he noticed—possibly out of deference to the dead girl. Conrad Miller was perched on a stool near the miniature bar, mixing one of his interminable drinks. He held up a rather unsteady hand in greeting.

"Hi, Inspector. Park yourself. Make yourself at home. What'll you have?"

Vandebona politely declined. "I'm on duty, sir. Now, if you don't mind, about that statement of yours—?"

Conrad Miller waved airily. The effect was marred by the fact that he waved with the hand that was holding the glass. Whisky and ice cubes slopped over the carpet.

"Look, you're not trying to hang a murder rap on me, are you?" he demanded. He half-rose from the stool. His face was flushed.

Eva Miller hurried to his side. "Nonsense, honey! The Inspector's here to help you. Now sit down and answer his questions like a good boy."

"All right, all right! But I don't see why the bloody hell he can't have a drink!"

Eva Miller sighed. She came forward with a bottle and glass.

44

"You'd better have one, Inspector. You'll find things easier with him that way."

"Sure, that's the stuff!" Miller exclaimed. "Now you're talking." He slid off the stool, handed Vandebona the soda siphon. He was in shirtsleeves and had on charcoal grey slacks and dark suede shoes. "Any friend of mine must drink with me." He raised his glass carefully. "Bottoms up!"

Vandebona gave an inward sigh of resignation. After all, he told himself, it was in the execution of duty. He raised his own glass.

Three whiskies and several cigarettes later Conrad Miller had unburdened himself of his second story.

He had gone to this bar in the Fort. He was real sorry he had misled the cops. The trouble was, if Heston knew he had been in the bar he would have taken a dim view of it. He'd been going there pretty regularly for some time. It was because of this thirst he had . . . They had no bar in the office, which was a pity. Now, if he had been the boss—

Anyway, he had decided to come clean. Yeah, Eva had told him it would be best if he did.

But he had a favour to ask. He would appreciate it if the cops kept the story to themselves and did not allow it to leak out to Heston. Heston was a good guy, but he was snooty where work was concerned.

Vandebona gave a guarded reply, designed to set the other's mind at ease. After all, if Miller was guilty of the murder he would have bigger things to worry about than his future with the firm. On the other hand, if he wasn't, there was nothing to worry about.

"Do you think you could show me exactly where the bar is?" he asked. He would have to check on Miller's story.

Miller agreed instantly. "Sure, I can. Only it's these local names that beat me. I could drop you at your office afterwards."

"That's very kind of you," said Vandebona. He set his glass down and rose. Mrs Miller came with them to the door.

"You be careful, honey," she warned her husband as he started the lilac-and-white Herald. "No more drinks, mind." She acknowledged Vandebona's wave. "Good night, Inspector. Drop in again some time."

Miller eased the car out into the lane.

"Bit of a noisy starter," he said. "There's an exhaust leak I've got to get fixed when I can find the time." He jerked a contemptuous thumb towards Allen's house as they went past it. "Not like that guy there. He's got the time—when he's not fiddling with his radio. Looks after his car like she's his wife."

He got on to the main road and turned left. Vandebona noticed that he was one of those drivers with instinctive reactions at the wheel, however much he might have drunk. Miller had automatically dipped his lights on the six-lane highway and was keeping to the left-hand lane. He was doing a steady twenty despite the temptation of the broad road with its thinning traffic. It was shortly after nine o'clock and the late theatre rush had not begun yet.

"About Eddie—" They had passed the traffic lights at the Kollupitiya junction and the elegant new concrete-and-glass headquarters of the British High Commission. Miller looked sideways at the inspector. "The cops are looking for him, aren't they? But he's no killer, that boy. He may have had a bit of fun with the girl, especially as it seems she wanted it, but that's about all. You mark my words, you cops have got to look some place else for the bastard who killed her. Besides, like I said earlier, Eddie's not been home since last night. He goes like that sometimes, to see friends, and nobody worries. He always comes back."

"But we've checked up with his friends, Mr Miller. He hasn't been to any of them."

"Sure, sure," Miller grunted. "But they were all the guys we knew. Maybe he's got other friends Eva and I don't know about. And another thing—although he's my stepson we've always got on well together. Maybe he appreciates that I've always let him have his own way. It doesn't do any good to repress a kid."

46

These modern young people and these modern parents, marvelled the conservative Vandebona. He knew what his father would have said—and done—if he had returned home late or committed the unpardonable crime of staying away for the night. Yet his father and he had been the best of friends. They had respected each other. He wondered whether he would have had the same respect for his father if he had let him have the freedom of the wild ass. That's what the younger generation were—a bunch of wild asses sowing a bunch of wild oats.

They were now passing the brightly lit expanse of the Galle Face Hotel on the left and now they had crossed the intersection and were on the sweeping stretch of the Galle Face Green.

On the right, just past the intersection, was the towering mass of the Walton, Ceylon's newest luxury hotel. The floodlit façade spread a glow over the night sky and its forecourt was crowded with gleaming, expensive cars. Vandebona sighed. Sexton Blake would be there with his beautiful secretary, perhaps in its exlusive penthouse night-club.

Out at sea the riding lights of ships were visible as they awaited their turn to enter the harbour. A cool breeze blew inland, laden with salt that settled lovingly on the metalwork of the cars that were parked on the Green with oblivious lovers. Gram sellers with kerosene flares and ice-cream vans with coloured electric jets were doing their usual brisk business. In the shadows, waiting for bigger profits, were the male and female prostitutes and their attendant pimps.

On the metalled promenade skirting the short drop to the beach portly businessmen were walking briskly in an optimistic ritual to become less portly. Children frolicked in sharply defined groups—the children of the well-to-do and the children of the nearby slums of Slave Island. The Green was no respecter of persons, Vandebona knew. It was for everybody and for everything—from romantic meetings to political rallies.

Vandebona became aware that Miller was speaking again.

"Of course, it might have something to do with that phone call Eddie got," he was saying.

Vandebona turned sharply. "Phone call? What phone call?"

"Didn't anyone tell you? Eddie got a phone call—must have been around one in the morning." Miller carefully negotiated the sharp, wrongly cambered curve near what had once been the exclusive Colombo Club and was now "Samudra", the Hotel School, training ground for the tourist drive the Island was belatedly planning.

He went on: "I don't think Eva got up, but I did. She sleeps in the next room and Eddie's room is across the corridor. I heard Eddie take the call so as soon as I knew it wasn't for Eva or me I went back to sleep. I'd no idea he was going out and maybe he didn't want to disturb us."

"Around one o'clock, you say?" Vandebona made a quick note. "We'll check on that. It could be important."

They drove on. Ahead of them, beyond the roundabout fronting the House of Representatives, loomed the clock tower at the Chatham Street intersection. Miller swung into a side street; he slowed down to a crawl and suddenly pointed.

Vandebona looked at the crowded bar. He knew the place. It was one of many such small bars in the side streets of the Fort. He reflected that Miller could hardly be blamed for not remembering the name. The garish neon sign over it said: "The Kapalla, Beepalla, Jollikorapalla Bar." The first word was in small lettering. What the sign blazed out was a Sinhalese transliteration of the phrase: "Eat, drink and be merry!"

"Better drop me here, Mr Miller," he said. "Thanks for telling me what you have told me. Good night."

"Going to do some checking up, eh?" grinned Miller. "You ask that fat slob behind the bar about me." He waited till Vandebona shut the door, then turned the Herald right round in the small space. "Be seeing you!"

He didn't know then that he wouldn't be seeing Vandebona again. Or anybody else. Not ever.

CHAPTER VII

Come Dark, Come Death

Night is the time for Death;
When all around is peace
James Montgomery: *Night*

CONRAD MILLER drove back home feeling, as he expressed it to himself, like a million.

It had been a mistake to try to pull a fast one on the cops. He had realised that the moment Eva had questioned him and pointed the fact out to him.

At the time he made his first statement he had been in a fix. He had to keep clear of Heston over his visit to the bar, for Heston did not like his staff drinking during office hours and was a stickler for discipline—a habit dating back to his Army days.

Well, now he had done it. It had been a brainwave to come clean with the inspector. He knew he could count on the guy not to let him down. Now Mr Robert Heston wouldn't know what wasn't good for him. He had nothing to worry about.

Unconsciously his foot pressed harder on the accelerator. The car surged past the Green. The cool breeze played soothingly on him.

To the left was the Walton and ahead, on the right, the Galle Face Hotel. Miller slowed down. He could do with a drink, he felt. Then he cursed. Just in time he remembered that he had promised Heston to call over at his place after dinner to discuss an important development that had arisen over the work project. Heston had specifically asked him to come as

Floyd was in no condition yet to attend to business matters. Vandebona's visit and the subsequent trip had completely put it out of his mind.

He glanced at his watch. Heck, it was nearly ten! The boss would be flaming mad. Well, he had the inspector's call as a genuine excuse. But no more drinks for him—not just yet, anyway.

His foot came down on the accelerator. The road was clear immediately in front of him, but to the right were the approaching lights of a double-decker bus with its trafficator signalling a right-hand turn. All buses had to make a detour there, past the United States Information Centre and the new headquarters of the Automobile Association of Ceylon.

The bus had the right of way. Miller's foot came off the accelerator pedal and pressed on the brake. The bus was about to take the turn, its trafficator still flashing. The car kept going forward. Miller's foot stamped on the brake again, harder. The pedal sank unyieldingly, right down to the floorboard.

The car went on.

There was an appalling crash as the double-decker ploughed right through it.

The insistent clamour of the telephone awoke Judy.

She heard Allen take the call. His voice reached her in a sleepy mumble. Then, suddenly, the tone changed. She heard a loud, horrified exclamation and a series of rapid questions.

The receiver was thrust back with a crash into its cradle and Allen hurried along the corridor. She heard him stop at the adjoining room, his quick, urgent knocking at the door and the excited exchange of words that followed between him and her father.

"What! *Dead*, did you say?" Floyd's voice came in shocked surprise.

"Yes. That inspector—Vandebona—was on the phone just now. Said he thought he'd inform us so that we might break the news to Eva. Conrad's dead—killed on the spot. A bus smashed right through his car."

Mary Floyd had come to the door. "What is it, Jeff? Who's dead?" And then: "Did you say Conrad? Oh, my God! Does—does Eva know?"

"Not yet. We were just about to—"

"Wait till I get something on. I'll come with you. Oh, that poor woman—"

Seconds later Judy heard her father at the door of her room. The doorknob rattled.

"She's locked herself in; sounds as though she's asleep. Good, no need to worry about her."

Judy listened to them descending the stairs. She heard the front door open and the click of the lock. She smiled. Dad was taking care that nobody could sneak in during their absence.

Well, they would be gone some time. This new tragedy was fitting in well with her plans. She drew aside the mosquito curtain and swung herself out of bed.

She unbolted the door and walked barefoot downstairs in her pyjamas into the hall. Dad had left the lights on there. She went into the dark study; the heavy curtains at the windows were drawn. She checked up on them before she switched on the light. Allen was, as she had expected, very methodical. Everything was neatly arranged. She went to the low, open bookshelf on the far side of the room and found what she wanted. It was a book with big, clear letters. She turned to the paper, paste and pair of scissors on the big writing table and started cutting out the letters she wanted, pasting them on a sheet of paper.

The clock on the wall said it was nearly eleven. She would have to say in her message "midnight tomorrow".

To make it quite clear she would make it read "midnight tomorrow, Sunday".

That would leave no doubt in the mind of the killer of her sister.

Freddie de Soysa got up in the morning feeling very much better. His tussle with the voice within him was fresh in his mind and now he found himself in full agreement with what that voice had said.

He performed his ablutions in the single dingy toilet that served the second floor of the block of tenements where he lived. He padded back in his bare feet to his room, removed his sarong and put on a sweat-stained beige shirt and a pair of jungle-green khaki trousers that were hanging from nails in the wall. His good pair of shoes was still wet, thanks to that blonde bitch at the Walton.

He let them remain where he had placed them, on sheets of paper to absorb the water. In any case, he wouldn't be wearing them with his present rig-out. He put on his other pair of shoes; they were cracked and down-at-heel but still serviceable. Their chief virtue, in Freddie's eyes, was that they were rubber-soled.

He folded his sarong and thrust it between the pillow and the mat on the wooden bed. Under the bed was the suitcase which normally contained his best suit. He felt resentful as he thought of that suit. He had handed it over to the dry-cleaners as soon as he had returned to his room the previous day.

That seemingly promising encounter in the hotel lounge had resulted in a drain on his slender resources. He had had to pay the taxi and he would have to pay the dry-cleaners.

Freddie de Soysa glowered as he combed his hair before the fly-specked mirror hung on one of the numerous nails in the wall. Sometimes he thought that only the nails held the place together. On an upturned packing case were a jar of hair cream, a tin of cheap talcum powder and a small bottle of coconut oil for his hair. The hair cream and the powder were for "big" occasions—like yesterday.

The more Freddie thought about the debacle in the hotel the more his resentment grew. The voice had been right; he owed it to himself to take his revenge on that girl for the humiliation —and expense—she had inflicted on him. At the same time he would cash in on whatever her employer might be doing.

Maybe, after all, yesterday's episode could be the turning

point of his life. It could lead him to big things. It might put him in the money—big money.

He wiped his comb on a rag, let himself out of the room, locked the door and picked his way hurriedly down the smelly stone stairs. A Tamil woman stood there, with heavy ear-rings that pulled down her ear-lobes almost to her shoulders and with brass ornaments in her nose and on her ankles. She was holding the hand of a squatting child and gave Freddie a bold, inviting smile. Freddie had to squeeze past, holding his breath.

He almost ran down the remaining steps into the heat and the crowds on the road below.

He would do anything, he thought—even commit murder— to get away from that hell-hole where he lived.

Dawn was breaking when Freddie de Soysa arrived at the Galle Face to begin his vigil.

Normally, he knew, the place was deserted at that hour but now, as he stepped off a bus opposite the old headquarters of the Automobile Association and made his way along the arcade past the U.S. Information Centre, he saw a crowd at the intersection ahead. Right across the road was a double-decker bus and, under the giant wheels, was the crushed and twisted wreckage of a car.

Freddie mingled with the crowd, glad of the cover they afforded. From their excited comments he gathered that the accident had occurred late last night.

"A *sudda* (white man) was in the car," a peon in white national dress was saying in Sinhalese, his eyes alight with morbid interest. "He was killed on the spot. The car was coming very fast. The *sudda* was drunk. He crashed into the bus."

"You are a big fool! Can't you see that the bus hit the car?" said a big, burly man who looked like a harbour labourer from his expensive palayakat sarong and nylon shirt. He looked menacingly at the little peon. The peon mumbled something to the effect that that was what he had heard on the way. Then he sidled off.

Freddie realised that the docker was right. Anyway, it didn't matter to him what had hit what. An urchin carrying a bundle of papers came up, shouting: "Gole Paish akshiden! Car dyvel *mala!* (killed)''. Freddie handed him fifteen cents and bought a copy of the *Ceylon Daily Sketch*. Splashed on the front page was the news of the crash, with a big close-up picture. There was also an inset of the man who had died. The peon, he found, had been right on one count. The victim was a *sudda*—an American named Conrad Miller.

The report said that Miller was a top technologist of World Power Ltd, the contracting firm for the big island-wide electrification scheme. It recalled that about twelve hours earlier the daughter of another key executive of the firm had been murdered in her house at Kollupitiya. It added that the inquest on Miller would be held later in the day. There was no suggestion of foul play.

But what attracted Freddie's attention was on the other page. There was a full-length, double-column picture of a virile-looking man with clean-cut features and dark hair; beside him was a singularly attractive girl in a two-piece suit. The picture was headlined: "Sexton Blake and his Secretary here.''

Freddie's heart gave a sudden leap. So this was Sexton Blake! He looked formidable, hardly a man to be trifled with. He read the brief caption. It said that Sexton Blake and his secretary, Miss Paula Dane, were in Ceylon on their way back to England from a mission in the Far East. Blake, it went on, had refused to talk about the assignment, but there were indications that it was one of considerable importance.

Freddie was disappointed at this lack of information. But at any rate, he knew now what Blake looked like. And he would find out why he was here.

He read the rest of the paper, including the small ads., in spells between keeping his eye on the Walton from amongst the crowd on the Green.

Gram sellers and vendors of tea, coffee and sherbet were doing brisk business. Freddie leaned against a lamp-post and munched boiled gram with which were mixed small cubes of coconut and pieces of dried chillies that made his eyes water and set his tongue on fire. He washed the gram down with tea delivered steaming hot from a portable urn. He let the tea cool before he could bring himself to swill it over his smarting tongue. The gram and the tea constituted his breakfast.

By eight o'clock, before the start of the rush hour, a break-down van had extricated the car and taken it away, a mis-shapen heap of metal. A driver of the Ceylon Transport Board drove the bus away, a uniformed constable beside him. The road was cleared.

At about nine o'clock a tall, well-dressed figure came out of the Walton and Freddie felt his heart-beat quicken. This was Sexton Blake! There was no mistaking him.

Blake walked up the road. Freddie, across the road, felt as though butterflies were having a jitterbug contest in his stomach. He looked away quickly as Blake glanced in his direction, but he soon realised that the other was only inter-ested in the obvious signs of the crash—the shattered glass like chips of ice on the road and the chalk marks made by the police. Then Freddie gave a sigh of relief as a taxi drew up at Blake's signal. He heard Blake say: "Fort."

He made no attempt to follow. Blake would come back, for Paula was not with him. Freddie walked into one of the shops in the arcade, asked for the use of the phone and dialled the Walton.

He asked for Miss Paula Dane.

"I believe she has gone to the swimming pool," came the smooth voice of the receptionist. "Shall I page her, Mr—?"

"It doesn't matter," said Freddie. He hung up.

That damned swimming pool again!

CHAPTER VIII

Brake it Easy

> *Ha! so stately!*
> *This sure will sink you.*
> Nathaniel Lee: *The Rival Queens*

THE INQUEST into the death of Conrad Miller was at eight in the morning. It was held in the room reserved for such purposes in the imposing new block in the General Hospital in Regent Street, Borella, one of the municipal wards on the eastern outskirts of Colombo.

Mrs Miller had insisted on being present. Allen had driven her the short distance. Heston had not come. He was busy seeing to the arrangements for the two funerals and also sending cables to Head Office in London.

Amongst the small crowd present at the inquest Allen saw Vandebona. He caught the other's eye and the CID man gave him a rather abstracted nod.

The coroner was a fussy little Muslim in an impeccable cream tussore suit and a black tie. He wore gold-rimmed glasses and an air of self-importance. The pen he was using to record the evidence was scratchy and every now and then he would swing it irritably over the bare cement floor.

On one side, in police custody, was the driver of the bus. He was a dark, big-made Sinhalese with black, bushy hair and eyebrows, blood-stained eyes and a half-open mouth through which showed betel-coloured teeth. He was wearing the khaki bush-jacket of the Ceylon Transport Board, a violent batik sarong and thick leather sandals. His name was Mudiyanselage Sadiris Appuhamy. He was looking completely indifferent.

Allen was the first witness to be called. For the second time in twenty-four hours he gave testimony of identification of a corpse. Next a police constable gave details of time and of measurements he had taken at the scene of the crash. He added that visibility at the time was good and that there had been no moisture on the road.

The medical evidence was then recorded. Eva Miller closed her eyes as the police doctor who had performed the autopsy went through his grisly catalogue.

Vandebona listened in grim dismay. Poor Miller hadn't stood a chance. Nor, he thought, would he himself have done if he had still been in the car.

A thin, balding man in a white satin drill suit with a grey tie was next called. He said he was Anura Rodrigo, an Examiner of Motor Vehicles. He had examined the bus and found it in good mechanical condition. The front tyres were good but the rear ones were slightly worn. The brakes were efficient.

The Herald involved in the accident was practically new and the odo-meter recorded only $3,014\frac{1}{4}$ miles. The tyres were new. The car could be expected to be one hundred per cent road-worthy. But there had been something radically wrong.

Anura Rodrigo paused and the coroner licked his lips, savouring what he knew was coming.

"I examined the brakes of the car," said Rodrigo, and suddenly a hush descended on the little courtroom. "The brake hose of the offside front wheel was leaking. At a certain stage it would have been impossible to stop the car suddenly in an emergency."

Beside him, Allen heard Mrs Miller give a little gasp. The coroner rapped on his table to still the excited murmur that had broken out.

"Quiet, please, everybody, or I shall have this court cleared." He addressed himself to the witness. "And in your opinion what would that mean, Mr Rodrigo?"

The answer came firmly. "It would mean, sir, that the

braking system was being gradually bled of the hydraulic fluid which maintained the pressure. A certain stage would be reached when there would be no reaction at all from the front offside brake shoes even to the maximum deflection of the brake pedal. It would then have been utterly impossible to stop the car. The handbrake would have been useless because it would act only on the rear wheels—even if the deceased had the time to think of using it."

"Could this state of the brake hose have been due to some mechanical failure?"

"Absolutely not, sir."

His next bit of evidence put the final touch to the courtroom drama.

"Then, in your opinion, Mr Rodrigo, what could have caused the failure?"

"The brake hose had been cut, sir. The cut is visible."

"Does that mean that some human agency was responsible?"

"Definitely, sir."

This was it! At last it was out, the appalling truth. The little shred of evidence that turned accident into murder. There was a sudden scurry as reporters hurried for the exit, their thoughts on inexorable deadlines and sensational headlines.

In vain the coroner tried to restore order. Through the hubbub Allen heard his voice: "In the circumstances this court discharges Mudiyanselage Sadiris Appuhamy and records an open verdict. The proceedings stand adjourned for a week to enable the police to make further inquiries."

There was a little gasp from Eva Miller. Allen turned to her.

She had fainted in her chair.

Somebody, thought Sexton Blake grimly, has been diabolically clever.

He was once more seated in the police chief's office. He had called to discuss the final plans for the rounding up of the dope gang, and had arrived shortly after nine o'clock. Herat had been in a hurry to settle the matter and Blake had wondered why. He knew as soon as the last detail of the plan had met with his approval.

"It's murder again, Mr Blake," said Herat. "This time the victim is Conrad Miller. And this time it's murder staged to look like an accident."

Blake heard him out in silence.

While Detective Chief Inspector Vandebona had been in Miller's house last night someone had cut a brake hose of Miller's car with deliberate intent to kill.

Luckily for the CID man Miller had driven slowly on the way out and there had been no need for him to do any hard braking. In any case, there would still have been sufficient pressure for the brakes to act. But all the while the precious hydraulic fluid had been oozing out. On the return journey the master cylinder would have been practically empty. The last few frantic jabs Miller would have made on the pedal would have squeezed out the remaining fluid.

If Miller had driven fast on the outward journey there might have been two corpses in the car. Vandebona was lucky indeed to have escaped.

The car had been out in the front of the house. All that was needed was a sharp knife.

"Who could have a murder motive against Miller?" demanded Herat. "Unless it was linked with the murder of Angela Floyd. Could he have come by some knowledge which was dangerous to the killer, do you think?"

"But Miller proved that he was miles away at the time Angela was killed," Blake pointed out. "There is no doubt about that?" He looked at Vandebona, who nodded.

"That's correct, sir. I checked up at the bar. Miller was there from 10.15 till 10.30 that morning."

Herat was persistent. "It might be that Miller later saw or heard something which made him a potential source of danger to the killer."

"That would seem to be the most likely solution," agreed Blake. "But it wouldn't be safe to bank on it."

"It provides the motive," said Herat quickly.

59

"Yes. On the other hand it is possible that Miller had no such knowledge. We can check on that from his movements. I think they will be covered by his statement and that of Mrs Miller." He glanced inquiringly at Vandebona.

The CID man took out a well-thumbed note-book from his coat pocket. He turned the pages swiftly. "Here we are," he said. "Miller came to Floyd's with the others about 11 a.m. He was there until the girl's body was removed, which was about two hours later. Then he went back home with Mrs Miller. They both lunched out, returned home about 3 p.m. Then he slept till past six and had a bath and until 7.45 he was at home, drinking, while Mrs Miller questioned him about his statement to us and persuaded him to tell the truth. Then she phoned me and I arrived there by eight. I was with him until shortly before he died."

Blake turned to Herat. "You see?—What chance had Miller to find out anything? I think you'll have to look elsewhere for the motive for his murder."

CHAPTER IX

Grave Venture

The Jabberwock with eyes of flame
Came whiffling through the bulgey wood,
And burbled as it came!
H. L. Dodgson: *Through the Looking Glass*

THE TWO FUNERALS had been held from the same funeral
parlour on that Sunday evening.

There had been a fair gathering—business friends, Judy
supposed. They were all strangers to her.

The simple grandeur of it all had impressed her. She had
been awestruck at the silent mourners, the beautiful wreaths
and the gleaming, luxuriously appointed Chrysler hearses.

As Angela's sister she felt she had a special place for herself.
The experience of being in the limelight had thrilled her. It
was the thing she liked most of all.

She had contrived to look melancholy and had walked at
Mum's side with downcast eyes. She had even let a tear trickle
down her cheek when the final prayer was said and the teak
casket containing Angela's body was lowered into the grave
amongst the jostling tombstones in the General Cemetery at
Kanatte.

She had looked just as solemn when Miller's remains
descended in their polished teak covering into their final resting
place alongside that of Angela.

Now it was all over, and she felt a sense of relief.

Despite Allen's protests Mary Floyd had changed her mind
and returned to their own home. She was now in her room,

with Jeffrey Floyd trying to comfort her. Judy was in her own room, adjoining theirs. It was the room she had shared with Angela.

Angela's bed was there, across the room, with its white mosquito net over it. Like the white shroud Angela had worn in her coffin. It was nearly nine o'clock now.

Three hours more to go, Judy reflected. She had sent her ultimatum to the killer—tonight, at midnight. That was the time she had set for the appointment. She must try to get some sleep first.

She had switched on the night-light. Through the communicating door came a faint glow. She heard her father come to the door.

"You all right, Judy?" His voice sounded strained.

"Yes, Dad. I'm sleepy."

He came into the room and crossed over to kiss her goodnight. "Good girl. You go to sleep now." His hands went around her tightly. There was an added warmth in his embrace and for the first time she realised how much she meant to him. Now all his love was for her. There was no Angela to share it.

She started to say something, but he had gone. He had drawn the mosquito net together and gone quietly from the room, shutting the door.

She wished she had confided in him. But now it was too late.

In the faint glow of the night light Angela's bed seemed to be staring at her, awaiting its occupant.

Judy turned the other way, towards the wall, and closed her eyes.

She couldn't sleep. Not at first. Not for what seemed an eternity of time. She tossed restlessly about on the soft mattress, her mind in a torment of fear, doubt and hope. She had an impulse to leap out of bed and run into the adjoining room, to pour the whole story out to her parents.

Should she go through with her plan? Would she succeed? Would the killer of her sister keep the midnight tryst? And what would happen then. Would things go the way she wanted? Or not?

She knew she was treading on dangerous ground. But if the killer tried any funny business, she would be ready. Thanks to her search in the Gregg boy's room she had a weapon which would stand her in good stead.

Of course, she wouldn't ask for too much to begin with. Later on, perhaps, she could increase her demands. Apart from the financial reward there was also the pleasure of knowing that she had somebody in her power; that she had the killer at her mercy. When all was said and done, she didn't really need the money. The whole thing was for kicks. What a story she would have to tell those stupid kids in the music class!

But that would be when it was all over. When she became tired of the whole thing and turned the killer over to the police. Would their faces be red!

And what a heroine she would be! She would be the central figure in a sensation that would rock the island. Her picture would be in all the papers. It might even appear in London, perhaps in the *News of the World*.

The little bedside clock told her that it was now a quarter to twelve. Quickly she pulled apart the mosquito net. She removed her pyjamas; under them she had on a pair of black jeans and a dark sweater. She thrust her feet into the rubber-soled shoes she had kept under the bed. And from under her pillow she took the torch and the other object she had hidden.

She peered into the adjoining room. It was dark now. Mum and Dad were fast asleep. She walked noiselessly out of her room, down the stairs and into the hall. She unlocked the main door quietly, pocketed the key in her jeans and went through the open gate and down the lane. She kept to the shadows cast by the coconut trees and the hedges on either side.

In one hand she held the torch. In the other was an air pistol—a toy, but deadly at close quarters.

Calixtus Pinto was looking forward to the end of his spell of night work—to the following evening, when he would be enjoying his daughter's birthday.

Florida would be four years old. She was the youngest of his seven children, and his favourite.

He had everything fixed for the party—from the cake with its lettering: "Happy Birthday, Darling Florida" to the short eats and ice cream for the little guests from neighbouring houses and the beer and arrack for the adults.

And there was the present he had bought for her. He had bought it that evening in one of the shops near the railway terminal at Maradana. It was in its daintily wrapped box in his locker in the cab of the speeding locomotive.

He smiled indulgently as he thought of Florida's treatment of dolls when she was quite small. She would tire of them after some time and break their limbs and throw them away. She still hadn't quite outgrown the urge to see what made them tick.

But this, he felt, was one doll she would treasure. It would be a memorable birthday for her, he told himself, as he peered through the oblong window before him, his hand on the regulator.

Ahead of him, bathed in the powerful glare of the headlight, the twin tracks stretched southwards until they were lost around another bend. Behind him trailed a line of freight cars. From the right, above the thunder of the locomotive, came the sound of the waves breaking against the giant boulders that lined the coastal stretch of railroad to Galle, the southern capital.

He had just passed Kollupitiya, a few miles from Colombo Fort. He enjoyed night driving and revelled in being on the footplate of a steam locomotive to the less noisome but less glamorous diesels.

The rush of salt-laden air increased as the old 4–6–0 put on more speed. The rhythmic clicking of the fast-moving pistons and connecting rods was like music in his ears.

Pinto had joined the Ceylon Government Railway straight from school and worked his way up from the bottom. But he still could not get over the boyhood thrill which the "Iron Horse" and the permanent way held for him. In a few years he would be retiring but it would be without regrets, for by then the steel monsters which had given such long service would be done away with and replaced entirely by diesels.

He nodded appreciatively as the fireman sounded the regulation warning whistle at the approach to the sharp bend ahead.

By noon he would complete the return run to Colombo. And then home, and Florida's birthday—

Abruptly he tugged at the whistle cord. From the clanking juggernaut came an ear-splitting banshee wail. It changed into short, sharp urgent blasts as the fireman took over the whistle cord from Pinto.

Pinto had other work to do then.

With his swarthy, coal-begrimed face suddenly bloodless, he pulled down on the throttle lever. The hiss of the suddenly applied vacuum brakes sounded like a million angry snakes. His hands worked frenziedly, obeying the frantic signals from his brain to do everything possible to bring the freight train to a halt before it was too late.

He did halt the train, short of sending it off the track.

But it could not do it quickly enough.

By the time the train had come to a shuddering, grinding stop it had passed over the little white body Pinto had seen on the line.

He jumped out, ran along the ballast with the fireman at his heels. They had to run along the length of the twenty-five heavily laden 21-ton wagons.

But the guard from the brake van at the rear was there first.

The guard did not have to run at all. He had only to step down and see what lay underneath and around the wheels of the brake van.

It was the mangled body of a little girl.

It was like a broken doll. Like a doll torn apart and flung away by a petulant child.

c

The sudden thought came screaming into Pinto's mind and his mouth was filled with the sourness of bile.

Like Florida, trying to see what made them tick . . .

While awaiting Blake's return Freddie de Soysa bought a copy of the *Evening Cry*. The tabloid splashed the news that the man who had died in the crash opposite where he stood had been the victim of a fiendishly contrived murder.

The paper linked it up with the murder of Angela Floyd and screamed the question: "Is there a hoodoo over power firm?"

Freddie grimaced. The tragedies were of no interest to him.

What worried him was how he could carry out his self-imposed mission. For the first time he realised the difficulties facing him. Keeping watch on the hotel was easy by daylight but when night came it would be difficult. Either Blake or Paula Dane or both could leave and he would be none the wiser.

Freddie thought of bribing one of the room boys, but decided against it. To begin with, he hadn't enough money. And, besides, the man might inform Blake or the hotel authorities and the police would set a trap for him. Even if he found someone co-operative enough he might lay himself open to blackmail.

Freddie, essentially a lone wolf in more ways than one, was still racking his fertile brain for ideas as night fell.

Blake had returned. Now he and his secretary were both in the hotel—and the moment of crisis had come.

Freddie walked across the road and stationed himself on the Green from where he could see the broad entrance to the circular drive of the Walton.

He bought ten cents' worth of boiled gram and stood munching it as he watched the cars drive in. They were opulent, well-maintained cars and the men and women in them were as opulent—though most of them, Freddie thought sourly, were not so well-preserved. They would be eating expensive food and dancing to hot music while he ate a poor man's food and shuffled his feet on the cold grass.

He had an equal right to be there, accepted as one of them, but for his past mistakes. He grew bitter at the thought. Then he brushed it away. He had the future to think of. It might be that the immediate future had something of advantage to him. It all depended on how he made use of his opportunities.

To his right the gravelled road leading to the promenade was also filling up with cars. They belonged to revellers who, Freddie knew, wanted to be sure of a quiet spot on the Green to which they could retire to end a hard day's night. The couples crossed the road to the Walton in laughing, chattering groups, the women in exotic saris and low-cut dresses; the men in formal evening attire or expensive lounge suits. Freddie knew that even his "best" suit was drab in comparison; anyway, it was with the dry-cleaners.

He jumped aside in alarm as a red Sunbeam Alpine bore down on him. Just in time the car swung into the side road, its front wheels bumping over the turf. It drew to a screeching stop and a woman got out hurriedly, slamming the door behind her. Her voice reached Freddie in an angry shout:

"You fool! Do you want to kill me? You've drunk more than enough and you're in no condition to drive. I'm taking a taxi back home!"

"Aw, what the hell, Sheila!" The man's voice was thick. He was making ineffectual efforts to get out of the low-slung car. "Shtop being a shpoilshport, will you? We're goin' to the Wal'on and then afterwards—"

"No!" The woman's voice was sharp. "You're not taking me there. I don't want to be seen with you while you're like that—you pig!"

She moved away, her stiletto heels clicking on the road. Her heavily-powdered, over-rouged face was flushed. She stormed past Freddie, not noticing him, her breasts heaving in her near-topless dress.

"Wait, Sheila!" The man was still trying to open the door. "Come back, you bloody bitch!"

The woman flung a snappy epithet at him. Even Freddie was taken aback by it. She hailed a passing taxi and hurled herself into its dark interior. The taxi was speeding down the Galle Road when the man got the door open and clambered out of the car. He stood swaying on the road, an owlish look on his face.

"Bloody—hic!—bitch!" he muttered. "I'll catch up with you!"

He turned to get into the car again. Then he collapsed as something hit him on the head.

Freddie deftly caught the falling body, pocketed the lead-tipped cosh and manoeuvred the unconscious man into the car. He got in from the other side and for the next few minutes he was very busy. When he had finished he was wearing the man's clothes and shoes. They fitted him to perfection. What was more satisfying still was that in the other's wallet were over a thousand rupees in notes.

His unconscious benefactor was now in his underwear. Freddie drove the car right down the short stretch of road and parked it near the end of the promenade. He flung his own clothes and shoes on to the beach below without any regrets. He knew that before long one of the night prowlers on the Green would make off with them.

He got off and walked to the Walton.

He found Sexton Blake and Paula Dane in the pent-house nightclub. The man from whom he had taken the clothes had booked a table; the reservation card was in the wallet. The table was for two, and Freddie explained to a suitably sympathetic head waiter that there had been a sudden and unforeseen change of plans which had necessitated his coming alone. No, he didn't want any of the hostesses for company. He preferred to be alone with his thoughts and the drinks.

The table was in a corner and he was confident that he would escape recognition, especially as the lighting was dim.

Blake and Paula were only a couple of tables away and they came close to Freddie when they took the floor again. Once more the sight of Blake gave him an uneasy feeling in the pit of his stomach.

Perhaps it was just as well for Freddie's peace of mind that he did not realise that Blake and Paula had picked him out instantly. Blake recognised him as the man who had been waiting outside the hotel and wondering how it was that the seedy-looking character of the morning had been transformed into a well-dressed guest at a top-price nightclub.

He commented on the phenomenon when the orchestra stopped playing and they returned to their table.

Paula glanced in Freddie's direction and her eyes widened.

"That's the man I told you about," she said. "The one I pushed into the swimming-pool. Freddie the Wolf. He looks lonely—maybe he's waiting for someone to turn up."

"Or something," said Blake reflectively.

Paula laughed. "His middle name must be Micawber."

Then she dismissed Freddie from her thoughts. She had other, more interesting things to think about. It wasn't often she had the chance of dining and dancing with her chief. She was determined to make the most of it.

It was Allen's unpleasant task once more to identify a body. He identified all that was left of Judy Floyd and was violently sick immediately afterwards.

And so the third inquest was held.

The medical evidence established that Judy Floyd had been mercifully dead before the train ran over her.

She had been strangled before her body was placed on the track.

CHAPTER X

Contract for Murder?

*Vice, then, it seems, is a fine thing
with an ugly name.*
George Berkeley: *Aleiphon*

"WELL, that's the score, Blake," said Heston. He wiped his face and the bald expanse on his head with a handkerchief steeped in eau-de-cologne and laid his shirt-sleeved arms on the glass-topped, nadun-and-teak desk. "Three murders in as many days. Two girls and a man—the man an employee of World Power and the girls children of another employee. And both of the men key people in the firm. It looks as if someone is making a dead set at us."

He looked at Blake, then went on: "I'm glad the big wheels at home had the sense to act on my suggestion. I saw your picture in the papers and cabled them, asking them to commission you."

Sexton Blake did not reply. He leaned back in the comfortable embrace of a heavily-upholstered chair in the air-conditioned office and his blue-grey eyes were thoughtful. It was almost as though he had not heard.

The man behind the desk looked appraisingly at him and thought with a pang that the detective did not seem to have changed at all since they had last met in the basement of a bombed-out building some miles out of Salerno during the Allied invasion of Italy.

Blake had then been on a top secret mission for a mysterious individual named Eustace Craille. He himself had been with a Commando division—Major Robert Heston; tough, lean as a greyhound and with a mop of unruly red hair. Well, all that remained of those physical attributes was the toughness. There certainly wasn't much left of the hair! He had let himself run to seed after he had landed the job with World Power Ltd, London, a few months after the end of the war.

His toughness had won him a top position. Then he had relaxed and taken things easy. A man like Sexton Blakc, of course, didn't have the time to take things easy. And Blake, come to think of it, wouldn't have the inclination to do so, anyway.

Even in his comfortable posture, with his legs crossed and a glass of whisky in one hand and a cigarette in the other, Blake looked like dynamite—relaxed dynamite, ready to go into action at any moment. Heston could sense the latent strength of his personality as though it were something solid and tangible.

The clean-cut features with their firm lips and the chin and jawline of a fighter; the high forehead, the tall, lithe figure with not an ounce of superfluous flesh—these instantly set Blake out as a man apart.

Merely looking at him Heston realised how much confidence the investigator could inspire. He could take a load of worries off a client's mind by his very presence.

"All right, Bob, a penny for your thoughts."

Heston let his face crease into a smile.

"I was thinking of the old days. Anyway, it's good to see you again."

"Strictly between you and me," said Blake, "I might have been tempted to ignore the cable your directors sent me from London this morning. But as I was on the spot, so to speak, and already know something about this shocking business, I have decided to accept the commission. It was a pleasant surprise to find you here—I had no ideas that the 'Heston' Inspector-General Herat mentioned, was you. Still, I'll do what I can."

"Thanks, Blake," said Heston gratefully.

Blake went on: "Now, what makes you think that somebody has such a grudge against World Power Ltd that it needs multiple murder—including the murder of two innocent young girls—to settle the score? Doesn't it sound rather—well far-fetched?"

But Blake knew very well that the idea was anything but far-fetched. He had had personal experience of the workings of Big Business and he knew that murder was a mere incidental in the unending battle for the power that money brings.* But he wasn't letting Heston know that he was aware of these things. He preferred to find out from Heston whether there were real grounds for his fears.

Heston rose to the bait. "Not in this instance, Blake. We landed this island-wide electrification contract with the Government in the face of competition from big combines from all over the world—some of them so big that they could buy us up ten times over and not feel the difference. We've made some pretty powerful enemies, I can tell you. And they're so ruthless they would stop at nothing—not even mass murder—to queer our pitch."

"But surely—"

"Hold on, I haven't finished yet." Heston took a hurried sip from his glass and stubbed his half-smoked cigarette in a chromium-plated ash-tray. "You're wondering how the murder of Miller and Floyd's two daughters could affect us. Well, Miller's death has robbed us of one of our top technologists. Despite his fondness for the bottle he was one of the most brilliant men there are on large-scale electrification. And the murder of Angela and Judy has turned Jeffrey Floyd into a shattered, nervous wreck who'll probably never recover from the blow. And he was a man who was Miller's equal in technical know-how."

Blake nodded sympathetically. Assuming that Heston was right, the murder of the two Floyd girls had been a master-stroke of devilish ingenuity. The deaths of two of World

*See *Slaying on the 16th Floor* by Arthur Maclean. S.B.L. No. 5.

Power's most valuable employees would undoubtedly have provided a motive and brought suspicion to bear, perhaps, on the party or parties involved; but at first glance it would seem that there was no possible connection between Miller's murder and the killing of Angela and Judy. Only Heston himself had suspected differently.

Heston went on: "You're wondering why the loss of Miller and Floyd is so important to us. There are thousands of skilled technologists. But Miller and Floyd set themselves up in a class of their own; something really unique. You see, the reason why we got this contract was that our tenders were fantastically low, thanks to those two. It was possible because they had perfected a new system that was going to be one of the big things of the century. It's utterly revolutionary and saves like hell on materials—therefore on time and money. And only Floyd and Miller knew the details.

"They were the brains. They had almost perfected their process when the chance came for this contract. We banked on them and made our quotations accordingly. It was a gamble, but it came off. By the time we had got through the formalities they had achieved success. But not all the results are down on paper. The key details were still in their heads. Now Miller is dead and Floyd is so cut up over the death of his daughters that I doubt if he'll ever be the same man again. And it could even be that our enemies—whoever they are—will get him too; just to make sure. He's our last hope now, and if anything should happen to him—"

Heston did not complete the sentence. He spread his hands out expressively.

"I see." Blake's voice was grimly reflective. He set his empty glass down on the low table beside him and pulled out a slim, monogrammed gold cigarette case from the pocket of his light grey tropical tweeds. He held out the case to Heston and they lit up. "What it boils down to is this: If anything should happen to Floyd as well, you stand to forfeit the contract and come a big financial cropper?"

"It would be the end of World Power Ltd, Blake. This thing

can make us or break us. You've got to find out who is behind all this—and stop them."

"Yes," said Blake. But he was thinking not so much of the enormous financial loss which World Power Ltd might suffer as a result of Miller's death and Floyd's near-breakdown, but of the hideous murder of two young girls. No matter what other—and greater—issues were at stake, he was ruthlessly determined to bring their killer to justice.

And he had to do it before the murderer killed again.

Sexton Blake stepped out on to the concrete foreground of the glaringly new, ultra-modern building on the sixth floor of which Heston had his suite of offices.

He had seen the layout of the place before he had left. It had given him plenty to think about.

Heston had explained to him that he had kept the private door to his own room open as the staff had not come. His door faced a small vestibule which led from the corridor that ran the length of the floor. The vestibule was bare. On its right was a door marked "Inquiries" which gave access to the main office. Immediately beyond the door was a reception hall with, on its left, the receptionist's desk. Behind the desk was a switchboard.

Heston had explained: "Mary Floyd is our receptionist as well as telephonist." He had pushed open a small gate in the wooden railing that spanned the passage between the wall on the left and the reception counter. In the space on the right were two extra-long tables strewn with blueprints. "This is where Floyd works—" he had pointed to the nearer table "—the other was Miller's. The desk at the far end is Allen's. He looks after the financial side."

On the far right-hand corner were two bathrooms. A door at the far left led into Heston's office. Facing it was a smaller door. Heston had opened it. The room it led into was narrow but neatly kept. It had an electric typewriter, a typist's swivelling chair and rows of filing cabinets.

"This is Eva Miller's room," Heston had said. "She's my secretary."

"Anybody else?"

"No. There's no chance of any outsider leaking out information."

It also narrowed down the field of suspects if there happened to be a traitor in the camp, thought Blake. He wondered how far World Power Ltd was justified in its fears. Probably the fears were groundless and the killing of Miller and the Floyd sisters had nothing whatever to do with the electrification contract. But he welcomed the chance of being in on the case officially. There was a mystery to be solved, and a particularly brutal killer to be laid by the heels.

He decided to see Vandebona and find out what progress the inspector had made. He knew that Vandebona would be delighted to find him working on the case and would give him full co-operation.

Blake looked around him. To his left was the clock-tower-cum-lighthouse at the Chatham Street intersection. The lighthouse had been replaced by a modern one at the seaward end of the nearby Galle Buck, but the clock still functioned. Its hands stood near ten.

The day was already uncomfortably warm. The business and shopping centre of Colombo presented a busy appearance with its constant stream of cars, taxis and second-hand double-decker buses. Some of the buses, Blake noticed with a nostalgic pang, still had their original London Transport Board number-plates and advertisements. One of the red giants lumbered past him with posters advertising a film that had run in Leicester Square six years ago. Another screamed "Fremlins". A third carried LLU registration plates.

The scene was a mixture of East and West. Apart from the obvious camera-festooned tourists and their obsequious guides and the hovering touts, there were Europeans holding top posts in commercial and State establishments. Mingling with them were a cross-section of the local population. Sinhalese and Tamils—the two major races in the small but strategically placed island—predominated. Their colouring ranged from black to golden-brown. Some were as fair as the Portuguese, the Dutch and the British who had ruled the island in turn.

The menfolk were mostly in open-necked shirts and slacks. The coat had vanished during the austerity years of the war, to be worn only for "occasions". Blake noticed quite a few of the "brown sahib" executive type in nylon shirts, narrow ties, rayon slacks and pointed shoes. The national-minded wore white cloth sarong-wise and long, flowing tunics with big slits in the sides for pockets.

Amongst the fair sex the sari-and-choli combination took pride of place and daubed the scene with splashes of gay colour. Blake saw that a surprising number of Burgher women—descendants of the Dutch and Portuguese—had adopted the garb. He thought it suited them, for he felt that this essentially Eastern form of attire was delightfully feminine. It spared the beholder the horrors inflicted by some mini-skirts.

Despite the ban on the import of cars imposed in 1960 there were, he saw, practically all the latest models on the road. One thing was almost totally absent from the scene, and for that he was thankful. There were very few rickshaws around. Blake had always considered it an undignified and degrading mode of conveyance—undignified for the rider and degrading for the human beast of burden between the shafts.

In place of the rickshaws there were taxis in plenty, scurrying about like so many black beetles with a total disregard for the rules of the road.

Blake had thought of walking to Police Headquarters. It was a short distance away past Queen's House, the residence of the Governor-General, and within a stone's throw of Gordon Gardens with its majestic status of Queen Victoria. But the heat put him off.

He hailed a passing taxi.

Paula Dane sat in the hotel lounge and sipped through a straw from a long, ice-packed glass of orange squash.

She had just had a refreshing half-hour in the swimming pool and changed into a cool white frock. Her long show-girl's legs were bare and on her feet were thin-soled leather sandals.

Admiring glances were bestowed on her from the males at the other tables, but if there were any wolves around they were keeping on their sheep's clothing, Paula thought. There was no sign of Freddie the Frightful, either.

Paula felt she had earned a rest. Putting together Blake's notes on their long chase after the dope gang and typing them in the form of a report to Interpol had been tough going. It had deprived her of the chance of going around, but she hadn't minded for she knew that Blake wanted the report urgently. Duty to her chief came before anything else. Now she had brought the report up to date and it remained only for Blake to return and supply her with the material for the closing chapter.

She glanced at her wrist-watch. And quite a few of the men in the lounge wondered who the lucky man was she was waiting for.

About noon they knew.

And then it was the turn of the women to sit up and take notice.

Even the men could not help taking a second look at the tall, lean, distinguished figure in the well-cut light tweeds who entered the foyer and stepped past the lounge towards the lifts with long, easy strides.

Paula caught his eye and stayed where she was. In a short while he was back. He had bathed and changed into a white silk open-necked shirt, cream slacks and moccasins.

"Sorry to have kept you waiting, Paula," he said as he sat down in the chair facing her. "Hope you've been enjoying yourself."

Paula grimaced. "Well, I've brought the report up to date, thank goodness. For the rest, I've been enjoying the view. Some day I'll write a book about the sun and the sea—and another about the sea and the sun."

Sexton Blake grinned at her and signalled a passing waiter.

"An iced Carlsberg—the colder the better," he ordered. He looked at Paula quizzically and she shook her head, her corn-flower-blue eyes twinkling.

They chatted desultorily until the waiter arrived. Blake

took an appreciative pull at the foaming mug. He offered his cigarette case to Paula and they lit up.

"Well, chief?" she asked presently.

Blake blew out a stream of smoke.

"It looks as though your enforced inactivity is about to end," he said.

Paula sat up alertly. her eyes sparkling with anticipation. Blake lowered his voice. He told her what Heston had told him.

"Sounds rather a tall order," remarked Paula when he had finished.

Blake nodded. "You can say that again. So far I've been in on this case in an unofficial capacity—merely to help our good friend Herat up to the time of our departure. Now we've been officially commissioned by World Power Ltd. This naturally puts paid to our flying back home tonight, so I've postponed our reservations for a few days. But you're free to go, of course, if you want to."

Paula looked indignant. "While you have all the fun?" Then she frowned and bit her lip. "I'm sorry—I didn't mean to sound facetious or callous. There's nothing to joke about in the murder of those two girls—or Miller."

Blake blew a perfect smoke-ring and watched it waft away into nothingness, caught by the busy overhead fans. "It's all right," he said. "I know what you mean. This case is going to be something to get our teeth into."

"What do we do first?" asked Paula.

"There's one thing I've done already, apart from cabling Tinker to let him know the change in plans. You see, Heston hadn't told the police about his firm's belief that the killings might be directed at them. After all, there is nothing tangible to go on; nothing at all. So far his theories are merely suppositions. But I persuaded him to inform Detective Chief Inspector Vandebona—you'll like "Bones", Paula; he's quite a nice chap and knows his job.

"Heston explained that he had been obeying instructions from his principals in London; apparently they didn't want to give their enemies any ideas in case their theory turned out to be completely off the rails. They've no desire to publicise that angle and thought there might be a leak through the police if they did so. I told him that the matter was now in my hands and that I considered he would be making a grave mistake if he withheld any kind of information from the authorities. He could request them to display the utmost discretion—which I'm sure they will."

He paused to pour more beer into his mug.

"Anyway, Heston phoned Vandebona in my presence and told him the whole story. That puts him—and us—right with the police. I don't want Herat or Vandebona to think I'm trying to steal a march on them. Now I can accept their co-operation with an easy mind. I've just had a chat with Vandebona—he's very happy that we're staying, after all."

"You still haven't said where we go from here," Paula pointed out.

Blake set the mug down; wiped froth from his lips with a spotless handkerchief. "Remember Richard Melder, my agent here?"

Paula nodded. She had seen the reports which Melder, like all Blake's agents abroad, sent monthly to the Berkeley Square office. It had struck her that Melder was a man who knew his job, like all the other agents. He had to.

"Well," Blake continued, "I rang him up on my way back and arranged for him to keep a watchful eye on Jeffrey Floyd. It's quite possible that, as Heston said, he could be in danger. Anyway, you'll be meeting Melder at Floyd's place; we'll be going there in a little while. Heston will be lunching with us here and then he'll take us. We'd better square up our bills and have our bags ready."

Freddie de Soysa was well pleased with his night's work.

He had returned to his room at four in the morning, and after a few hours' sleep he was back at his post. He had put on a pair of old, baggy flannels and a soiled shirt. His feet were thrust into his rubber-soled shoes.

About nine o'clock he saw Sexton Blake leave in a taxi. By

noon Blake was back. And then, about an hour later, Freddie saw Blake and Paula get into an Austin A55 drawn up under the wide concrete porch of the Walton. A couple of uniformed porters followed and began piling luggage into the boot. This was it!

Tingling with excitement Freddie stopped a taxi, got in, and asked the man to wait. When the A55 swung out into the road the taxi was behind it. A European was at the wheel of the Austin and Freddie realised why his face had seemed familiar when he glanced at the day's *Daily Sketch*.

As on the previous day he had whiled away part of the time by going through the morning paper. It splashed the news of the murder of Judy Floyd and the inquest verdict on the death of Conrad Miller. It linked the two murders with the death of Angela Floyd and laid heavy stress on the fact that all three victims were connected with World Power Ltd. It echoed the question the *Evening Cry* had asked: "WHAT IS THE JINX OVER WORLD POWER?"

Despite himself, Freddie—an ardent crime fan—had been interested. He had read every word of the sensational report. And he had looked closely at the picture of the chief representative of the firm, Robert Heston. The man who was driving the A55 had seemed to resemble Heston, but he couldn't be sure.

They went only a short distance. Just past the traffic lights at the Kollupitaya junction the car turned into a lane on the right. Freddie stopped the taxi, paid his fare, and got on to the pavement. He could see down the length of the lane; like most of the lanes on the seaward side it was a cul-de-sac.

But what intrigued Freddie most was the name of the lane. There it was, in its Sinhalese, Tamil and English lettering: Kumudu Mawata. This was the lane, according to the newspapers, in which the man Miller and the two Floyd girls had been living. He had been right about the driver of the A55 being Heston, then.

But, above all, he had achieved success in the first part of his self-appointed task.

Now he knew what Blake's mission was!

He ducked into an eating-house. He was feeling hungry and he also had had plenty of food for thought. He would satisfy his inner man and keep an eye on the lane while he thought things over.

The eating-house was crowded and filled with the clatter of plates and the shouted orders of perspiring "waiters" in sleeveless gauze banians and tucked-up sarongs. Freddie was fortunate in getting a table which gave him an excellent view of the mouth of the lane.

He ordered rice and curry and for once, though he was ravenously hungry, he did not mind the delay. The longer he waited there the better. He hoped, however, that Blake would not come out again before he finished his meal.

Sharing the imitation-marble-topped table with him was a seedy-looking clerk in frayed shirt and trousers who was reading the evening paper while waiting for his food. The clerk was engrossed in the sports news. Freddie looked at the front page, which was turned towards him, and his heart gave a jolt.

The front page carried a banner headline. It said: "Rs. 30,000 reward for killer!"

Freddie leaned forward and eagerly scanned the newsprint. The *Evening Cry*, "true to its reputation of being Ceylon's brightest and most go-ahead newspaper," was offering the reward for the apprehension of the "Mystery Slayer of Murder Lane", or for any information leading to the arrest.

That was all the story had to say, really. The rest was merely a re-hash of what he had read in the morning paper. But that was good enough for him. He could do with that thirty thousand!

Now, more than ever, it was imperative that he should keep an eye on Sexton Blake. Through Blake he might get a lucky lead.

The food arrived but now Freddie merely toyed with it, his hunger forgotten. He was filled with a bigger hunger—for thirty thousand rupees.

CHAPTER XI

Tree of Knowledge

'*Of Man's first disobedience, and the fruit
Of that forbidden tree.*'
Milton: *Paradise Lost.*

SEXTON BLAKE'S first move after Paula and he had been
installed in the Floyd household was to visit the school compound at the end of the lane.

Mary Floyd, a worn, shadowy-eyed wreck of a woman, had
welcomed him with tears in her eyes. Her confidence in him
had touched him deeply.

"Mr Blake," she had said, making a brave effort at com-
posure, "We have lost our two beloved daughters, and there is
nothing that can bring them back. But I beg you, with all my
heart, to get the fiend who killed them."

Jeffrey Floyd cut in harshly: "The *Evening Cry* is offering a
big reward to whoever discovers the killer. I can't match that,
but I'll give everything I possess if you can avenge the death of
my two girls."

"I'll do my best," said Blake quietly. "As for the question
of a reward, I shall consider it sufficient reward to get my
hands on the murderer. And now you can help me make a
start by telling me everything you know—every little thing,
however unimportant it may seem."

But although he questioned them closely, trying to get hold
of something that would give him a starting-point, they could
think of nothing out of the ordinary.

"One thing," said Floyd presently, "Judy's death would seem to prove that it isn't Eddie who is the killer. He might have killed Angela—in a fit of passion, though I find it very hard to believe he could do such a thing—but he couldn't possibly have killed Judy. There's been no sign of him, has there, since—since Angela's death?"

"No," said Blake. "We're working on a telephone call he received that night—or in the early hours of the morning, rather. If we can trace the caller it might give us some clue to his whereabouts."

Blake had examined the girls' room, going through it minutely with Paula's help. The only fact that emerged was that Judy had gone of her own accord to meet the killer, or had been enticed to her death. Her pyjamas still lay on the floor by her bed, flung over her slippers.

"She had put on a dark sweater and jeans and rubber shoes," said Floyd. "She must have left when we were asleep. I had kissed her goodnight—" A spasm contorted his face and he turned away quickly. He recovered himself with an effort and went on: "She must have taken the front door-key with her. She had also taken a small torch and an air pistol which Gregg's son—one of her classmates—had identified as belonging to him. They were found on the track, together with the key."

"When did the Gregg boy miss his air-gun?" Blake asked.

"Why, on the day of Angela's—" Floyd's voice broke again, but once more he succeeded in mastering his emotion. "You see, Gregg is a friend of ours who lives along the main road. His son and daughter attend the same school as Judy. She was there that day and I asked Gregg to take her back to his place when he called for his children. I brought her back in the evening and we all slept at Allen's house."

"And it was while you were there that you heard of Miller's death?"

"That's right. Allen, Mary and I went across immediately to Eva Miller. Mary and I stayed with her, and Allen went to the scene of the crash."

"And Judy?"

"She was asleep. She had locked her bedroom door. But I locked the front door too, just to be on the safe side, and took the key. We were away for about a couple of hours, until Allen came back with the police. He stayed until they took down Mrs Miller's statement."

"And when you returned to Allen's place the front door was still locked?"

"Yes. And Judy's room, too. She was still asleep—we didn't want to disturb her, anyway."

There was nothing the Floyds could add to that.

Blake had also inspected the sun porch and the hall leading off from it. Both had been cleaned up and still smelt of colour-wash and disinfectant. Whatever clues they might have yielded had been wiped out.

Now Blake was at the spot where Judy had gone to meet her death at the hands of a killer. The police had found ample evidence of a struggle near the little wooden gate of the school-house. But since then the sandy soil had been trampled over and over by an army of morbid sightseers.

Nevertheless, Blake examined everything with his customary thoroughness. He was not surprised when he failed to find anything useful. There were no broken buttons or torn pieces of clothing obligingly left behind by the murderer.

There would be nothing to gain by an inspection of the rail tracks, either, he reflected.

He wiped his face with his handkerchief. He had changed into shirt and slacks again; the heat was still oppressive though it was now past five in the evening.

He paused to look at the magnificent mango tree that stood between the windowless side wall of the schoolroom and the gate. He smiled to himself as he saw scrape marks on the thick trunk. It was not the season for the succulent, juicy fruits, but that had evidently not deterred some young climber.

He went up to the tree. And then his blue-grey eyes narrowed as he looked past it and down the lane.

He came to a sudden decision. With a swift, athletic heave

he caught an overhanging bough and swung himself into the main fork of the tree.

He spent some time amongst the branches. Then he lowered himself back to the ground and on his face was an air of quiet satisfaction.

As he dropped to the ground beneath the tree a scream rent the air. It came from immediately behind him.

Blake turned. A woman was standing there, and was just opening her mouth to emit another scream.

Blake put on his most charming smile and said quickly: "I'm sorry if I startled you—"

Her mouth was still open, but Blake's smile and matter-of-fact voice reassured her. The second scream, to his relief, died stillborn. Instead, he was favoured with a faint, hesitant smile.

"You did startle me!" Now that she had got over the shock she spoke severely. It wasn't often that Emily Syms had the chance of admonishing an adult, and she made the most of the opportunity—especially as she instinctively sensed that he was what she classified as a "nice" man, and that there would be no come-back.

"What were you doing up that tree?" she demanded. "And who are you?"

Blake told her who he was. In any event, she would know his identity soon enough from her neighbours.

"It was the mangoes," he explained. "I've always had a liking for them. I didn't realise, of course, that they wouldn't be ripe. I'm afraid I had my climb for nothing—"

She looked at him chidingly now. "You men!" she said. "You're like naughty children." Then his name seemed to register with her and her mouth dropped again. "Did you say Sexton Blake?" she breathed. "The detective? Then you must be here to find out who killed those two poor girls—and Mr Miller. You must come home with me, Mr Blake, and meet my sister, Bella. I'm Emily Syms. I teach music here, but we haven't had any classes since those dreadful tragedies and I don't know when we shall start again. Not that I mind, for to tell you the truth I'm glad of the rest. I can still feel the effects of that terrible headache I had the morning Angela Floyd was killed. Can you believe it—I was actually resting in my office at the time?"

She pointed to the small, red-tiled building. "Every time I go there now I shall remember that. But I had to come today to remove my music sheets before somebody stole them—or the rats ate them. They're such a nuisance, you know—almost as bad as the crows. And such big ones, too—you wouldn't believe the noise they make, scampering about in the attic. They quite frighten me, though Bella doesn't seem to mind them in the least."

They had been walking up the lane as Emily Syms went on with her monologue. Blake made no attempt to stem the flood. In all that verbal flotsam there might be something of value to him. He had, despite her protests, relieved her of the burden of carrying the bulky pile of music sheets and books.

Emily Syms paused near a wooden gate with broken hinges. "Won't you come in, Mr Blake?"

"I'd be delighted," said Blake.

He followed her up a short gravelled drive through what had once been a garden but was now a jungle of weeds. The house was a relic of the colonial days. Like most old houses by the sea, it had no verandah but was completely enclosed for protection against monsoon weather. It was single-storeyed and high-roofed, with two small dormer windows. The whitewash on the walls was peeling off and the red paint on the doors and windows had been blistered by the sun and blackened by coal dust and the salt-laden air.

"You'll have to excuse the state of the garden," Emily Syms told Blake. "I simply haven't the time to attend to it, what with the teaching and the cooking and having to look after Bella, poor dear. And we have to go once a week to the Pettah to buy our groceries—such an awful area though it's so near the Fort! We go by bus, of course, because we have no car and we do not like to trouble the others—not that they would mind obliging us, especially that nice Mr Allen, bless him, though last week I

86

found myself wishing that we had a car when I found that Bella was suddenly missing. But luckily we had arranged where we should meet if we got lost in those awful crowds, and there she was, like on the previous week, quite safe, and as cross as two sticks because she said I'd wandered off and left her, when it was the other way round . . . Well, here we are." She dug into one of the pockets of her long dress and brought out a bunch of keys.

She unlocked the door. Blake followed her into a large, gloomy hall which was sparsely furnished. Immediately ahead was a flight of stairs. Emily switched on the light.

She locked the door behind her. On the left was a wide archway leading into what seemed to be a lounge.

"Bella must be resting," she said, and pressed a switch near the arch. A light sprang to life in the inner room, leaving most of it in shadow. She motioned Blake in. "Please be seated, Mr Blake. I won't be long."

She took the bundle of papers from him and turned back into the hall. Blake watched her going upstairs.

"Bella!" she called. "Yoo-hoo, Bella! We have a visitor. Guess who?"

Her voice trailed away. Blake did not enter the lounge immediately, but went to the door at the far end, his feet noiseless on the worn carpet. The door was padlocked. A door facing a cupboard under the staircase led into a pantry-cum-kitchen littered with piles of unwashed crockery. That much he could see in the fading light between the stout planks nailed across two small windows. On the right of the hall and opposite the archway was another door, but that too was padlocked.

Blake went into the lounge. He took a deep breath. It looked more like a junk shop than a drawing-room; cluttered with an amazing assortment of furniture, most of it decrepit.

At the far end, in what was evidently the place of honour, was a big sofa with carved legs and torn upholstery through which showed tufts of hair stuffing. It was flanked by a rocking-chair and an old-fashioned whatnot. The rest of the space was taken up by a large wooden chest and chairs.

On the left were two large windows with heavy iron bars across them, but they had evidently not been opened for some time for the room smelt musty. The air was stifling and Blake found himself sweating. He picked his way gingerly across to the windows and tried to open them, but the big iron bolts had rusted in their sockets and would not budge. Wiping his forehead, he went back, trying to find a serviceable chair on which to sit.

The chairs were dusty and not very clean; in sharp contrast was the sideboard behind the sofa. It was spotlessly clean, as though somebody had dusted it lovingly every day. It had three shelves but the lower ones were bare. The top shelf depicted a battlefield in miniature. On the wall above it were framed portraits of Churchill, Eisenhower and Montgomery.

Blake examined the miniatures with interest. They were something more than a child's collection. He had never seen anything quite like it outside a war museum. Deployed on the shelf were metal replicas of a modern army in full battle-grey.

There were infantrymen, paratroopers and sappers. There were convoys of lorries with men and supplies; tanks, field-guns and machine-gun emplacements; an airfield complete with fighter planes, bombers with the RAF insignia, gliders, Red Cross vans, staff cars, jeeps and every other form of mechanised transport. It was all realistically laid out, down to buildings made of cardboard, a railway, and roads and rivers painted on the contoured plasticine surface.

It was, Blake thought, an extraordinary thing to find in the home of two middleaged spinsters.

"You like it, Mr Blake?"

He turned sharply. A woman with plump features and a big, sagging body was looking at him from the doorway. She came into the room, followed by Emily.

"I think it is very interesting," said Blake as he walked across to her and took the proferred hand. "Does it belong to you?"

"It has become my life's work," she said, and her eyes gleamed in her smooth face. "I am Bella Syms. My sister has told me about you, Mr Blake. I am sorry I kept you waiting. I was meditating and must have fallen asleep. We are so glad to have you. The police here are efficient, but——"

She gave a genteel shrug. Blake noticed the small plastic plug in her ear, with a long cord leading down to her dress pocket. She caught the direction of his glance and smiled apologetically.

"You'll pardon this rather cumbersome thing, I'm sure. I'm deaf, you know—quite deaf without it. But I only use it in conversation; the batteries don't last very long and are not always easy to get." She went on: "Won't you please be seated?"

Emily fluttered around Blake. "Please do sit down," she said. "I suppose you want to question us about those dreadful murders."

Bella said: "With such terribly goings-on it wouldn't surprise me if all of us were murdered in our beds. But I've taken the precaution of seeing that no-one can enter *this* house. There is only one way of getting in, and that is through the front door. Emily sees that it is always locked—What is it, Emily?" She turned quickly as there came a small gasp from her sister.

Emily was raising a hand to her mouth. "It's nothing, Bella dear. I knocked my wrist against a chair. I'm so sorry, Mr Blake. It's this light . . ."

Bella Syms resumed her interrupted progress. She went to the sofa and sat down, smoothing out her voluminous skirt. Emily sank into the rocking chair. Blake selected the cleanest-looking of the chairs and sat down rather gingerly, hoping it wouldn't collapse beneath him.

CHAPTER XII

There's Many a Slip

The best-laid plans of mice and men
Gang aft agley.

Burns: *To a Mouse.*

"As a matter of fact," said Blake to Paula afterwards, "I might just as well have addressed my questions to the sideboard or the sofa. They told me absolutely nothing. Bella says she never saw, or heard, a thing; it seems that when she's on her own she switches off her deaf-aid; which is logical, I suppose. Yet I've a feeling . . ." His voice trailed off and he stood a moment looking into space while Paula watched him intently.

He had just finished telling her about his encounter with the sisters Syms. It had taken over an hour (plus a cup of steaming hot coffee which tasted as though brewed from sunflower seeds) and a limp and perspiring Blake had finally taken his leave of them with profound thankfulness. He had returned to Floyd's house for a bath and a change of clothes before doing justice to the excellent dinner Mary Floyd had prepared, with Paula's expert help.

Now he and Paula were in the study. "You were saying you had a feeling, chief?" she prompted.

"A feeling that Emily Syms knows something. Unfortunately she chatters at such speed and is so easily confused that whatever she does say cannot always be taken at face value. Also, she seems to be somewhat intimidated by Bella. I think perhaps you'd better take over the questioning tomorrow, Paula. By the way, I wonder when Melder—" He broke off as a car drew up outside.

"Perhaps that's him now," said Paula quickly.

The doorbell rang. They went out of the study and into the lounge as Mary Floyd opened the front door.

The man who entered was dark, with a weatherbeaten face. He was bigly built, and he had on a fawn-coloured suit with a white shirt, dark tie and tan brogue shoes. His face crinkled into a smile as he saw Blake and Paula.

"I hope I'm not late, Mr Blake. I've been looking forward to meeting you and Miss Dane." He shook hands with them warmly. "I'm sorry I missed you both—and Tinker—when you were here last time. I'd have been glad to help any way I could."

Blake smiled back at him. "Well, neither Paula nor I knew we were in on that particular case until the end." He introduced his agent to the Floyds. "You've got a chance to be of some help now," he told Melder. "That's why I got you down here. Let's be seated, shall we?"

While Floyd saw to the drinks, Blake looked thoughtfully at Melder across the lounge. Melder was engaged in conversation with Paula, who seemed to have taken an instant liking to him. Blake smiled to himself. Paula was an excellent judge of character and he had considerable faith in that judgment. Melder was one of his most recent acquisitions abroad; he had been an inspector in the Special Branch of the Ceylon CID but had resigned because he disliked political interference.

"Big crime here", he had written to Blake, bitterly, "is now big politics. You've got to toe the line—or else."

That had been towards the middle of 1964, shortly after the unholy alliance which the then pro-leftist Government had formed with the Marxist groups in an abortive attempt to crush the democratic parties. In the following year Melder had gone to England for a special course of training at Scotland Yard. Blake had met him at a conference there.

They had kept up a desultory correspondence after Melder's

return to Ceylon, shortly afterwards. Then Melder had informed him that he was quitting the Force and setting up a private Enquiry Agency ("no divorce cases, Mr Blake—just good clean crime"). Blake had appointed him some months later, as one of his South-East Asian agents. He knew that Melder had got a terrific kick out of the appointment and was determined to prove his worth. So far, except for his usual monthly reports, he hadn't had a chance of doing so. But now the chance had come.

Blake helped himself to brandy from the bottle Floyd handed him. He wondered whether to drink it. He would have preferred something long and well-iced. Though it was nearly nine the night was warm and sultry. He thought longingly of the sea nearby; maybe tomorrow he would take time off for a swim. He was sure that Paula would welcome the idea.

He took a sip of the brandy and set the glass down.

"Well, Richard, this is how you can help," he said, looking at Melder. He told him that it was important that the Floyds should be taken to a safe place and well guarded.

"It should only be for a few days," he said. "That will leave my hands free for the main job."

Melder nodded. "Naturally I appreciate you couldn't give me any details over the phone. But I got the general idea. I've arranged everything, Mr Blake."

"Good man!" said Blake. "Where is the place?"

"It's on a coconut estate off Negombo. That's just past the Katunayake International Airport and about an hour's drive from here. The estate belongs to a friend of mine who's a crack racing driver." Melder coughed. "People say that kasippu— that's the local brand of hooch—is distilled there. The point is, the place is guarded day and night. And the estate bungalow is one hundred percent modern. It's got everything—from sound-proofing to the latest in bathroom fittings. You will have a pleasant stay there, Mr Floyd. If you'll excuse me saying so, I think both you and your wife appear to be badly in need of a change of surroundings."

Blake nodded his appreciation of the point. He knew what

effect the empty house, which had once rung with the voices and laughter of the two young girls, must be having on their parents. He turned to Mary and Jeffrey Floyd, who were seated together on the settee. They were listening, their eyes troubled. During dinner, earlier on, he had informed them of his proposed plan, but it had not been easy to convince Floyd. He had been obstinate—vehemently so.

"I want to get the swine who killed my girls!" he had declared. "I don't want to be hiding away somewhere. If you think I'm in danger—fine! I'll set myself up as a target. I'd welcome it. Just give me the chance, that's all."

Blake had pointed out that such an idea would not be practicable. It sounded all right in theory; it happened in books and on the films, but it didn't work out like that in real life. It might come off—then again, it might not. The chances were that it might not—and he wasn't prepared to take that chance.

He had told Floyd that they shouldn't overlook the possibility that the killer was someone well known to them and in their confidence; somebody who could easily get past their defences. Besides, it was a negative approach to the problem. What he wanted was a direct approach and for that he wanted his hands free.

Blake was quietly insistent, and in the end Floyd had agreed.

"We'd better get our things ready, Mary," he said now. He helped her to her feet and led her upstairs to their room. They came down shortly afterwards, Floyd carrying a suitcase in each hand. He set them down in the lounge, and gave Blake a tight-lipped smile.

"All right, we're on our way," he said.

"You can count on Mr Blake, Mrs Floyd," said Paula, as she looked into the grief-ravaged face of the bereaved woman. "He'll do everything he can, I assure you."

Mary Floyd managed a wan smile and followed her husband to the door. Blake and Paula went with them to Melder's car, which was drawn up under the porch.

"I'll report back, Mr Blake," Melder said.

Floyd helped his wife into the car, then got in himself. He thrust his face out of the window.

"Find the murdering swine soon, Mr Blake," he said.

Melder nodded goodbye. Blake watched the car drive up the lane, then he walked back into the house with Paula beside him.

He was looking very thoughtful. A growing sense of uneasiness was preying on his mind.

CHAPTER XIII

The Indiscreet Sea

The sea is silent, the sea is discreet,
Deep it lies at thy very feet.
　　　Longfellow: *The Golden Legend.*

PAULA WAS QUICK to sense Blake's changed mood.

"What's wrong, chief?" she asked.

Blake was leaning on the low surround of the porch on which Angela Floyd had met her death. Lotus Lane lay bathed in darkness, except for a faint light which showed high up from the Syms sisters' house.

"Sorry, Paula. I'm rather worried. No, not about our main problem. That's what makes it worse, in a way."

"What is it, then?"

"That's the devil of it! I don't know. I just can't place it."

"*I* know," said Paula. "It's this heat. It gets you down." She glanced at the printed dress she was wearing over the barest essentials. "It's so sticky. There's not a breath of wind, not even blowing in from the sea."

Blake stood up suddenly. "Well, if the breeze refuses to come from the sea we could breeze down to the sea. Care to come?"

"Watch me!"

They went into their respective rooms—Paula had been given the main room and Blake the guest room—changed into bathing kit under their clothes, and walked down the lane. Blake first took the precaution of locking up the house and hiding the front door key under a flower-pot. He left the lights on.

The light in the Syms' house showed weakly from behind an upstairs window. Evidently one of the sisters preferred to have a night light. Blake wondered if it was Emily and whether it was because of the rats in the attic.

There was no moon but the faint starlight was sufficient for Blake and Paula to find their way to the end of the lane and across the rail tracks to the beach, over the huge blocks of granite placed there to prevent erosion. The sea was calm.

Paula gave a delighted cry and let drop the brief skirt she was wearing over her bathing-suit. She ran across the narrow, sloping strip of sand and waded in. Blake slipped off his slacks and followed leisurely.

Paula slid her lithe body into the water and as she swam she remembered a day in Honolulu; another little island, another golden beach and swaying palms—and the blue waters of the Pacific. And a swim which would have ended in death for her but for the kiss of life given to her by Sexton Blake.*

That was the first time she had felt his lips on hers. It was a memory she would always cherish. The experience had been worth the near-tragedy.

She let herself drift with her thoughts, pleasurably.

She thought she heard Blake call out to her and smiled to herself. Let him come after her! Perhaps she could pretend to be drowning and he could save her, as he had done last time. She laughed mischievously.

Her arms and legs moved with the perfect timing of the skilled swimmer. She was about a quarter of a mile from the shore now. A few hundred yards away she could see the long, jagged reef and the white-topped breakers.

She turned back. She decided to head towards the tip of the little headland on her left. She saw Blake some distance behind her, swimming strongly. This time she heard him call out—it sounded like a warning. Well, there was nothing to be afraid of; she wasn't going out to the reef. She was going back now, anyway.

She would swim back along the curve of the headland. She

_____

*See *The Last Tiger* by W. A. Ballinger (S.B.L. 4th series No. 526).

increased the rhythm of her movements. She could see the out-thrust arm of the headland more clearly now in the starlight. It ended in a rocky formation and as she drew closer she could see that it was riddled with small openings and caves, hollowed out by the waves.

The openings were awash. The sea burst into them and fell back, frothing and roaring, as if with baffled fury. Paula turned away. She could hear Blake clearly now:

"Paula! You had better come back!"

"It's all right, chief. I'm fine—Ouch!" Paula gave an involuntary gasp as she felt her foot catch in something. She tried to kick herself free but the movement caused an agonising pain to shoot through her leg. It appeared to be trapped in something; some object that enmeshed it. The harder she tried to break away from it the more she found her leg was entangled.

The pain increased; Paula stopped struggling and called out to Blake. She tried to keep her voice steady.

"Chief—over here! Can you come? Please hurry!"

In a moment, it seemed, he was at her side. He did not waste time asking questions. Her pain-twisted features told him all he needed to know.

"Hang on, Paula," he said.

He jack-knifed through the water. Paula felt his strong hands on her leg. Suddenly the terrible constriction around it eased and she gave a little gasp of relief. Blake reappeared near her.

"It's all right," he told her. "Think you can get back on your own?"

Something in his voice set the alarm bells ringing in her mind. "Of course," she said. Her leg was sheer hell as the salt water took over. "What is it? What trapped me?"

"It's a roll of thick wire mesh. It's broken away and one end is sticking out. There's something at the other end—"

He dived in again. This time he took longer to come up, and then his face was very grim.

"There's a body rolled up in the mesh—or what's left of a body. Get back to the house as fast as you can and contact the police. If possible, get Vandebona."

97

Paula turned and set off for the shore, without wasting any more time in words. Every movement of her injured leg hurt but she gritted her teeth against the pain and hurried. She found the going over the granite boulders even more difficult, but she finally made it and got on to the ballast bordering the railway tracks. She didn't want to keep Blake waiting out there longer than she could help with a corpse for company.

She set one foot on the nearest sleeper.

Then she jumped back as a bright light fell on her. It would have blinded her if she had not instinctively turned her face away in time. She fell sprawling on the ballast as a train came round the bend on her left and hurtled past her.

She felt the terrible slipstream and put her hands to her eyes to shield them from the stones and particles of grit that were flung up by the pounding, swift-moving wheels. The ground beneath her vibrated and she was almost deafened.

Her body trembled with shock. But for that quick leap backwards she would have shared the fate that had befallen Judy Floyd—with this difference; that she would have been alive when the train struck her. The thunder of the sea had drowned its approach—and later she was to learn that literally scores of tragedies had occurred along that stretch of track for that very reason.

Now the train had gone. Paula raised herself cautiously. Her body was a mass of bruises and covered with coal dust, and her leg throbbed with pain. Hurriedly but using the utmost care to see that the tracks were quite clear, she crossed over to the opposite side, limping.

She passed the dark shapes of the little school and the house of the two Syms sisters. The night light was still on, she noticed. On her right loomed the gates of Floyd's house. She raised a dirt-streaked hand to open the latch.

Then she gave a startled exclamation and swung round. She heard a sound from the hedge bordering the lane and glimpsed a dark figure rushing towards her with something in its up-raised hand. She caught a glimpse of what she took to be an iron bar. She tried to move away but her injured leg hindered her. At the same time it helped her, for she stumbled violently and the blow that had been meant for her head fell upon her shoulder. It was a hard blow, bringing her to her knees. She fell forward on the metalled surface of the lane.

Dimly she heard a savage exclamation of triumph as the figure bent over her. She saw the iron bar descending again but was powerless to move.

This, she thought, is the end.

Her last conscious thought was of Blake. She had let him down.

Richard Melder did not take the obvious route out of Colombo, through the Fort. He was too old a hand for that. True, there had been no signs of pursuit in the lane, but if anybody wanted to keep track of Floyd's movements away from the house they would have a look-out at the top of the lane and be in a position to follow him in the flow of traffic on the main road without arousing suspicion.

So Melder turned right instead of left. He swung into the main stream. There wasn't much traffic about and he ignored speed limits as he sped down the best and broadest trunk road in Ceylon.

At the next junction, Bambalapitiya, the traffic lights showed red. Melder cut into the left-hand lane and, with tyres screaming, got into the broad stretch of New Buller's Road. Now he could really let the Humber go! At the Buller's Road Junction he crashed through the traffic lights and the speedometer hovered between sixty and seventy as he went down the long, straight, tree-lined thoroughfare with its palatial, old-world mansions and its modern offices and houses. Time was when only cars were permitted along it. But conditions has changed. Like most of the surrounding 'high society' Cinnamon Gardens area, it was now a bus route.

He passed the silent, ghostly buildings of the Forensic and Technical Branches of the CID and it was only when he reached the next intersection that he relaxed. If there had been any pursuit he had shaken it off; his rear-view mirror told him that. At a sedate twenty he turned left opposite the General Cemetery at Kanatte into the narrow, congested road leading to the nearby bus terminus at Borella.

He passed the five-armed junction, went down the straight stretch of Baseline Road. At Serpentine Road he made a detour past the Colombo Oval and climbed back to Baseline Road along the steep little road (beloved of driving instructors and examiners) within sight of the forbidding walls of the remand jail at Welikade.

He turned right. He had made quite sure that he was not being followed. He went over the level crossing, thankful that the gates were open and that he would not have to wait for one of the slow-moving 'baby' trains of the narrow gauge railway to Ratnapura, the city of gems. Further down where the main tracks of the broad gauge railway led northwards, he was held up, but the electrically-operated barrier did not keep him waiting long.

Quite soon he was at the end of the narrow, rut-strewn road and on the broad dual carriageway leading to the new bridge over the Kelani River. At the end of the bridge he got on to the main Kandy road, turned left and went the short distance to near the old Victoria Bridge, where he swung right into the Negombo road.

Beside him, Floyd was seated, chain-smoking. Mary Floyd was in the rear. Now safely out of Colombo, she suddenly broke the silence, forcing herself to speak, Melder reflected.

"I've been on this road a few times," she said. "We came along this road from the airport when we landed here. Now we go there to see friends coming in or going off. And we've been to the rest-house by the sea at Negombo."

Melder nodded. Negombo's claim to fame lay in its prawns and crabs and at the rest-house one got them fresh from the sea. He dipped the lights of the Humber to overtake a double-decker which was emitting dense clouds of black smoke from its exhaust. He cursed. The police, he knew, had been threatening for years to take action against "belching" buses but nothing had been done—or looked like being done.

"I'm sure you enjoyed the food there," Melder remarked as he went past the bus.

Floyd spoke for the first time. He threw away a half-smoked cigarette. "Angela and Judy, too, enjoyed the fish," he said. His voice was harsh, ugly.

Melder's hands tightened on the wheel as he heard Mary Floyd give a rasping sob. Floyd turned round in his seat and caught her hands.

"Sorry, darling. Please forgive me. It just slipped out—"

They drove on in an uncomfortable silence.

The road surface was pre-mixed and the Humber ate up the miles effortlessly. They sped round a wide bend into Wattala, a rapidly expanding suburb fringed by the beach at Uswetakei-yawa, the smugglers' paradise which the Government planned to turn into a tourists' paradise.

There was still plenty of night traffic and Melder had to slacken speed for the next four miles as the road narrowed and twisted. Then came the broad, open section at Mattumagala before the road again narrowed and squeezed through the townships of Kandana and Ja-Ela.

They crossed the narrow, single-lane bridge over the murky and crocodile-infested waters of the Dandugama Oya, flashed through Seeduwa and the turn-off to the International Airport at Katunayake. Negombo was only a few miles away, but the main road skirted the town.

Melder drove over the level crossing at the northern end.

"We're almost there," he said.

He covered a couple of miles, then turned into a narrow branch road that wound through a forest of coconut trees. On one side was a thick hedge but the other was fenced in by barbed wire to a height of about fifteen feet. The posts were of concrete.

Melder stopped at an iron-barred gate. Two men in sarongs and singlets came out from a watch hut. Both were dark, squat, powerful and both carried shotguns. A torch flashed on the car, its beam coming to rest on Melder's face.

"Ah, mahatmaya, it's you," said one of the men in Sinhalese. "We were told to expect you." He switched off the torch and spat out a chew of betel. He unlocked the gate and Melder drove down a well-kept, tree-lined drive.

The headlights lit up the endless, symmetrical rows of the tall, slender coconut trees and the fallen branches that, when dried and soaked, would be woven into cadjans to thatch village huts. There were also piles of husks waiting to be turned into coir fibre, and there were enormous mounds of husked nuts which would provide copra, coconut oil and desiccated coconut. This was the region in which had reigned the "copra barons" before prices had slumped to rock-bottom during the depression of the Thirties.

The drive passed through a large, well-tended flower garden and ended under the portico of a modernistic bungalow which was blazing with lights. As Melder braked the car and cut the engine a white-saronged figure appeared on the steps of the long verandah.

"Ayu bowan, Podi Singho," Melder greeted the man in Sinhalese. He explained to his passengers: "That's the servant boy." Then, to the white-saronged figure again: "Where's the master?"

The "boy" came down the steps. He was short, wizened, and about fifty. He was grinning widely, showing betel-stained teeth in his dark face. His eyes were bright and alert.

Melder was helping Mary Floyd to alight.

"The master, he has gone to Kandy," replied the "boy" in English. "He told to tell you and the *sudu hamu* to take the full liberties with the house."

"Thank you, Podi Singho," said Melder. He spoke in English and the "boy" beamed. "So the master has gone to Kandy, eh? Well, he told me that he might be away on business. Will you please bring the suitcases?"

He unlocked the luggage boot and took the two visitors into the sumptuously furnished hall. An enormous radiogram and a cocktail bar were amongst the accessories.

He escorted the Floyds down a long, thickly carpeted passage and opened one of the doors that led off it.

"This is your room," he said. "You won't be disturbed here. Every one of the rooms is sound-proofed. That is one of my friend's little fads. He has a house in Colombo and uses this place only when he wants to relax. And he hates being disturbed when he's resting, so he had his room sound-proofed. He's extended the same courtesy to the guest rooms."

The room was exquisitely furnished, with a big double bed and a colour motif of palest cream and eggshell blue. There would certainly seem to be money in the kasippu business, if what was said of their absent host was true, thought Jeffrey Floyd.

They entered the room, closely followed by Podi Singho, who placed the suitcases on a low rack. At a sign from Melder he withdrew, flashing a smile at Mary.

"Goodnight, missy. If you want anything pliss ring the bell there. You comfortable, no? There is no flea in the ointment?"

"No, Podi Singho," she replied, wrenching her mind back to their immediate surroundings. "Everything is quite all right. Thank you and goodnight."

He bowed his way out, closing the door behind him.

Melder looked at his watch. Despite the detour through Bambalapitiya he had taken the fastest route out of Colombo. He had done the trip in even time.

"Well, it's time I left, too," he said. "You will be well looked after here—and quite safe."

"Just a moment," said Floyd, stepping towards him. "Suppose something does happen? Supposing somebody gets wind that I'm here and slips past the guards? I can't just be looking on, you know. And there's my wife. Shouldn't we have something to protect ourselves, just in case? A weapon of some kind?"

Melder laughed. "Nothing can happen to you here, Mr Floyd. And I'll be dropping in daily until Mr Blake says it's safe for you to return home. It's my guess you won't have to wait long, with him handling the case."

"The case," repeated Mary Floyd bitterly. "I suppose that's

all it is to anybody else—just a 'case'." She put her head down in her hands and began to cry, hopelessly.

Floyd put one hand on her shoulder, but he was still looking at Melder. There was an obstinate expression on his face.

"I'd prefer to be safe than sorry," he said. "If you've got a gun—"

Melder shrugged. "Well, if that's the way you feel about it, you'd better have mine. I have a spare one back at the office. You can return this to me afterwards. It's a Colt automatic." He took the flat gun from his shoulder holster and handed it to Floyd. "Be careful, it's fully loaded. You're pulling back the safety catch—!"

"That's right." Floyd's voice was strained. He was pointing the gun at Melder. "If Blake and you think I'm going to stay cooped up here you're mistaken, both of you! I'm going to get the fiend who killed my girls. I've done a lot of thinking over the past couple of days and there's something I want to check up on." He jerked the gun. "If what I suspect turns out to be true, then this will come in very useful—"

Melder took a step forward.

"Stop where you are!" Floyd warned him. "I'd hate to have to use this on you."

"Think of your wife!" urged Melder.

"I am thinking about her," said Floyd. "You did quite right to bring her here. But not me. I propose operating on my own. Don't worry—I shan't get in Blake's way."

He looked at the white-faced woman standing beside him.

"I'm sorry, Mary, but you do see, don't you? I can't sit here twiddling my thumbs while that devil who killed Angela and Judy is still at large. Don't worry about me. I'll be quite all right. I'll get in touch with you the moment I can—" He backed towards the door, still levelling the gun. "All right, Mr Melder—you were in a hurry to be going. So am I. After you."

Mary had been standing as though petrified, but now she sprang forward with a cry:

"Jeff! You can't do this!"

"I can and I will. Nobody is going to stop me."

"Then I'm coming with you." There was a note of quiet determination in her voice.

"Don't be foolish, Mary! You'll be quite all right here."

"I won't stay here alone! It's . . . it's heartless and cruel of you to leave me this way!"

"I can't take you with me. You'd be in the way."

"Then take me back home. At least I'll be amongst friends."

He glared at her for a moment, then his expression softened. "All right, Mary, I'll get Melder to drop you back at the house. Get the suitcases—"

She obeyed and all three of them walked towards the door, Mary behind Floyd, Melder in front. His hand was on the doorknob; he had only to open the door a fraction and shout an alarm.

Something in the stiffening of his shoulders must have told Floyd of his intention. The barrel of the gun descended on the nape of Melder's neck before he knew what was happening, and the world seemed to explode. He was unconscious before he hit the carpet.

Mary gave a cry of horror. She dropped the suitcases and made to run forward, but Floyd checked her.

"Don't worry. He'll be all right, apart from a headache. I didn't want him yelling his head off the moment he opened the door. We'd have had a horde of servants here in no time. Ring that bell by the bed—"

She obeyed wordlessly. Floyd pocketed the gun and opened the door. Podi Singho appeared in a surprisingly short space of time and his eyes threatened to come out of their sockets as they saw the sprawled body of Melder.

Floyd spoke to him urgently. "It is his heart," he said. He motioned to his chest and the "boy" nodded vigorously, eager to show that he understood. "We must get him to the doctor. Help me to carry him."

Floyd bent and lifted the unconscious inquiry agent beneath the armpits. The servant, taking his cue, grasped Melder's legs. Together they carried their burden to the waiting car. They put him carefully in the deep rear seat and Mary got into the front with the suitcases.

"Thank you, Podi Singho." Floyd pulled out a ten-rupee note and handed it to him. "When your master comes back, please tell him what happened."

The man took the note then glanced from Floyd to Mary in obvious bewilderment. "But the missy—she remain—" he began.

"We'll be back later perhaps," said Floyd, cutting short the man's expostulations. "In the meantime, thank your master for us when he returns."

The servant salaamed. "I will tell. You take this master to hospital soon. I will phone men at gate to have gate open for you. Master come back soon, no? Cheerio, missy!"

CHAPTER XIV

Murder Rock

Great Neptune, hear a swain!
His coffin take.
    William Brown of Tavistock:
        Britannia's Pastorals.

SEXTON BLAKE knew that he was in for a fairly long vigil.

It would take Paula at least three-quarters of an hour to get to the house, and perhaps another hour for the police to arrive.

There was no point in waiting in the water. He swam to the narrow strip of shingle near the tip of the cove and paced up and down, for there was a distinct nip in the night air now. His feet sank into the soft sand, and his long, lean figure was etched in the starlight.

On one side was the dark mass of the little cliff overhanging the beach. On the other, the sea kept up its monstrous, monotonous refrain. Away to the right a train flashed past, its long line of lighted windows glaring like yellow eyes through the darkness.

Blake wished he had a cigarette, but he was wearing only his trunks. He glanced at his wrist-watch; the illuminated, waterproofed dial showed him that an hour had passed. There was at least another half-hour to wait.

He walked up and down for a while, for it was beginning to turn a little chilly, then sat down on a loose rock. As he did so he heard faint sounds overhead. He wondered if the police had come sooner than he had expected and got up quickly. The movement saved his life. The heavy boulder which had come tumbling down the cliff hurtled past him and buried itself with a thud in the sand.

Shielding his head against the hail of small stones which came in the wake of the boulder, Blake ran up the beach and took refuge under an overhang. He waited there, tense and watchful, but no more missiles followed.

Had it been an accident? Had some freak of the wind that was now blowing in from the sea dislodged the boulder? Or had some human agency been responsible? If the latter was the case, Blake knew it would be futile to attempt to climb the cliff to find out. He would present an easy target—and a helpless one.

Nevertheless, he felt certain it was no trick of the wind that had dislodged the boulder. It would have taken a wind of near-hurricane force to have done so. That meant somebody had been up there on the cliff-top; was probably still there, wondering if he had succeeded in his deadly mission.

Carefully, using every inch of cover and keeping to the shadows, Blake worked his way along the base of the cliff to where it tapered out to sea. To one of his mountaineering skill, climbing the cliff was child's play. He reached the top, drew himself gradually over, careful not to show himself against the skyline. He lay amongst some tussocks of wind-whipped grass and peered into the gloom.

Faintly, very faintly, he heard the sound of rapidly receding footsteps. He leapt up and hurried forward in pursuit, but the unknown had too much of a start. If Blake had been familiar with the terrain he might have been able to close in; as it was he was further hampered by his bare feet for neither he nor Paula had bothered to put on their shoes.

Luck was obviously on the side of the unknown.

But there was a question in Blake's mind. Why had the would-be killer not gone down onto the beach to find out if Blake had been killed by the falling rock? Was it that he had taken it for granted that the attempt had been successful? And why had that attempt been made? To prevent public disclosure of the dead body enmeshed in the wire?

In that case—

Paula!

The thought struck Blake with the force of a physical blow. It hammered into his mind with sickening significance.

What had happened to Paula?

Had she reached the lane safely—or had she come face to face with the killer?

It was very likely, for the only access to the beach in that particular area was along the lane. Paula would have been going up it and the killer would have been coming down. They could not have failed to have met.

Was that the reason the murderer had rushed back from the cliff-top after the attempt to kill Blake? To establish an alibi?

Moreover, the police had not yet arrived and there had now been ample time for Paula to have summoned them. Unless—

Sexton Blake hurried forward now with a growing sense of urgency. Heedless of the pain of his bruised feet upon the granite blocks and rubble, he made his way to the tracks and ran across them towards the lane.

He was still running when he reached Floyd's house.

Under the porch was a black Austin A30. He wondered whose it was. He ran to the front door, thrust it open, and burst into the lounge. Voices came from the study. He thrust aside the curtains—then came to an abrupt halt on the threshold.

Jeffrey Floyd gave a grin of satisfaction as he saw that the gates were open. True to his word, Podi Singho had telephoned to the watch hut.

Beside him, Mary sat in a terrified silence. He slowed down. It wouldn't do to arouse suspicion by being in too much of a hurry. The two watchers were standing near the gates and Floyd noted with further satisfaction that they did not have their guns with them.

He drew abreast of them and stopped. He made an urgent gesture towards the rear seat. The men peered in through the window and saw the recumbent form of Melder. They drew back, concern showing in their swarthy faces. Evidently Podi Singho had told them of Melder's "heart" condition, probably with some trimmings.

Floyd gave a tight-lipped nod, waved to them and shifted into second gear. He let in the clutch. As the car passed the gates he heard the sound of breaking glass and looked back. Melder's heavy brogues were jutting through the rear panel. In a second they were withdrawn. Melder had now struggled into a sitting posture and put his head out through the window. Floyd heard him call out to the men in Sinhalese.

His foot came down hard on the accelerator as he took the left-hand turn past the gates and the sudden swerve flung Melder back onto the seat. Floyd spoke to him through clench-ed teeth:

"All right, Melder—just stay there. Don't try any more funny stuff. And don't try jumping me from behind. Remember, I'm driving."

He was sending the car hurtling towards the main road.

"I'm not trying anything." Melder's voice came to him evenly. "I'm not forgetting that Mrs Floyd is also in the car. If you've any sense at all, you'll turn back."

Melder was still feeling groggy. But he was thankful that he had recovered sufficiently in time to give the alarm to the men at the gates.

Luckily for Floyd they had left their guns in the hut, other-wise they would have shot at the tyres and brought the car to a halt. But by the time they had run into the hut for their weapons it would have been too late. Floyd's get-away had been too swift.

Now, thought Melder, he must keep Floyd talking, prevent him from concentrating fully on his driving. He had to gain time. He was mentally kicking himself for having failed in his duty; for having let Blake down on this, his first assignment. But there was still a chance of saving the situation.

So he kept on talking to Floyd—pleading, cajoling. In Mary he had a good ally.

They were now on the main road, heading back towards Colombo.

"Look, Mr Floyd," said Melder, making a final desperate plea, "Let's go to the rest-house, have a drink, then get back to the estate where we can talk things over. I'm sure when you've had time to think things over—" His voice trailed away: Floyd was not even listening.

Ahead of them was the branch road leading to the town of Negombo. Melder stole another glance through the back window. There was hardly any traffic. Far behind, he saw the twin pinpoints of approaching headlights. He redoubled his efforts.

"Take that turning to the town, Mr Floyd. We can relax there and come back quietly. Let Mr Blake handle things for you. He's best qualified for the job. It isn't fair on your wife—"

Mary Floyd turned an anxious face to her husband. "He's right, Jeffrey. Please do as he says. Mr Blake will be very angry."

"I can't help that." Floyd spoke curtly. "Let him go ahead his own way. I'm going mine. One or the other of us will get that killer—and I hope it's me. I think I know who it is—"

"Jeffrey! You know?" Mary's voice rose in astonishment.

"I said *I think* I know. I've got to do some checking-up before I can be sure. And I'm not going back to that hide-out, so you can both save your breath. Leave me alone, will you?"

There was utter finality in his voice. The speed of the Humber increased. Soon they were past Negombo and approaching Katunayake. Floyd had settled himself down to driving in earnest. The powerful headlights lit up the deserted road.

Melder glanced back again. The pinpoints of light behind had grown and now he could make out the dark shape of the car which was following them. It was closing in rapidly. In the driving mirror Floyd saw the approaching lights and trod harder on the accelerator.

"It's no use, Mr Floyd." Melder spoke quietly. There was now a note of triumph in his voice which was not lost on the other.

"What the hell do you mean?" Floyd took a bend with tyres screaming.

"You might as well stop. The car behind you is an E-type Jaguar which my friend uses for racing. I told you he's a crack racing driver, didn't I? He's not at the wheel now, but his driver, Yapa, is about as good. He's going to overtake you—better let him get ahead, then pull up behind him."

The car was dipping its headlights repeatedly. Floyd slammed the accelerator pedal down to the floorboard. Mary gave a little scream as the car leapt forward. Hedges and houses flashed past in a blur. The road rushed to meet the hurtling monster.

Mary Floyd tried to speak, but the wind caught the terrified whisper that came from her and flung it away. Around and behind her was an inferno of screaming, snarling sound. She closed her eyes and held tightly to the door jamb as the car careered around corners. She found herself praying.

Behind her, Melder was shouting: "Stop it, man! You can't do it!"

Floyd was driving as though possessed by the devil—or as though the devil were after him. He had rocketed through the sleeping village of Seeduwa. Now the road was lined with giant mara trees, and ahead was the S-bend over the Dandugama Oye bridge. Floyd changed down and took the first bend.

The headlights showed a double-bullock cart at the other end of the single-lane bridge. The cart was almost at the entrance to it. Floyd didn't hesitate. Still in gear, he roared down the bumpy surface of the bridge.

Mary had opened her eyes. She wished that she hadn't. She shivered as she saw the steel girders flashing past and stared in terror at the approaching cart with its towering load of cadjans. In that moment she really believed that her husband had gone mad.

Then the car had swung past the lumbering cart and she heard the swish of the cadjans as they scraped its side.

The cart hadn't stopped. Melder knew from past experience that no self-respecting carter would make way for anything on the road. One cart on a bridge would sometimes cause a mile-long traffic jam. And at night most carters dozed or slept while they let the bulls amble along on their own.

And this was one of them, he knew.

He knew it when, shortly afterwards, he heard the scream of tortured brakes and the sound of a terrific crash.

He twisted back in his seat. The Jaguar had hit the cart. The car, the two bulls and the wreckage of the cart were sprawled in a confused heap across the mouth of the narrow bridge. Spread liberally and impartially over and around them were heaps of cadjans.

Jeffrey Floyd drove on in silence. Mary lay slumped in her seat. Melder was cursing to himself. If it wasn't for Mary he would have tried to wrest control of the car from Floyd.

He was angry with himself for having let Blake down. Thanks to that bullock cart his hopes of stopping Floyd had receded. Now he was really on the debit side with Blake—unless he pulled off something before the end of the journey.

But Floyd didn't give him a chance. Within half an hour they were re-crossing the new bridge over the Kelani and had re-entered Colombo. At the Borella junction Floyd turned down Ward Place, the Harley Street of Ceylon, and twisted through the maze of Lipton's Circus into the broad stretch of Turret Road. Near the war memorial at the end of the Vihara Maha Devi Park he drew the car to a halt. It was a secluded spot. He got out, carrying one of the suitcases.

Mary cried: "I'm coming with you, Jeff!"

"No, darling." Floyd had crossed around the front of the car to her side. She had also alighted and was standing on the kerb with her bag. Melder had ranged himself beside her. Floyd pointed the gun at him.

"All right now! That was just a trick to get you out. I need the car. I'm sorry about this, Mary, but its something I have to do on my own." Still covering Melder, he backed to the door, which Mary had left open, and slithered along the upholstery to the driving seat. He reached out a hand and closed the door.

He had to pocket the gun to start the car and drive away. This was the chance Melder had been waiting for. He could still turn the tables on Floyd.

He jumped forward. Then he stopped, wincing, as something hit him hard on the shin. Mary was swinging her suitcase menacingly.

"Leave him alone!" she snapped. "He's a right to do as he pleases. He's not your prisoner."

The car sped away. Still nursing his shin, Melder groaned.

This, clearly, was not his lucky day.

Minutes later, he hailed a passing taxi. There was no point in trying to follow Floyd. In any case, what Mary had said was true enough—he had no authority to stop him from doing whatever he wanted to do. He only hoped it would not be something too foolish; something which would decrease Sexton Blake's chances of solving the murder riddles.

Melder helped Mary to the taxi and clambered in beside the driver. Floyd's house was not very far away. He gave the directions.

They drove straight up past the Liberty Cinema to Kollupitiya junction, turned left at the traffic lights and were presently at the mouth of Lotus Lane.

The lights of the taxi lit up the road. Preoccupied with his own thoughts. Melder caught only a fleeting glimpse of the dark figure that sprang back into the shelter of the hedge. Then his eyes focused on the near-naked form that lay sprawled near the gate of Floyd's house.

The driver had seen it, too, and sent the taxi hurtling down the lane. He drew up with a jolt and Melder sprang out. Mary followed him.

Gently Melder turned the limp form over.

"Good heavens!" he gasped. "It's Paula Dane!"

Sexton Blake swung back the curtains and stepped into the

study. "What's been happening, Melder?" he rasped.

At the sound of his voice Paula opened her eyes.

"Hello, chief!"

She smiled wanly and tried to raise her head from a pile of cushions. The white-suited, professional-looking man beside her made a disapproving noise.

Blake reached Paula's side in two long strides, concern in every line of his face. "All right, Paula, take it easy," he said gently.

She lowered her head obediently back on to the cushions. The movement sent pain shooting through her injured shoulder. She was lying on a divan, covered with a blanket; it had slipped from the upper part of her body and Blake saw that, like himself, she was still in bathing kit. The exposed flesh was scratched and covered with dirt. There was congealed blood on the ankle which showed over the edge of the divan and bruises on her hands and arms.

Blake turned hard and accusing eyes on Melder and Mary Floyd. Melder he had expected to see, but the sight of Mary set the alarm bells clamouring in his mind.

"What happened?" he demanded. "And what is Mrs Floyd doing here? Where is Floyd?"

Melder told him. Blake waved aside his apologies. It was not Melder who was to blame; it was himself. He was filled with a terrible anger. Everything had gone wrong, right from the very start. Now he realised why he had been so worried after Floyd had left; he had had a feeling that the other man was proposing some move of his own. A move which might very well take him into the danger Blake had tried to avoid for him.

But his first concern was for Paula. He turned to the little man in white, Dr Ralph Misso, the Floyd's family doctor.

"How is she, doctor?"

Dr Misso pursed his lips. In all his fifty-three years of well-ordered existence he had never encountered such violent goings-on. He was essentially a family doctor, used to dealing with common household ailments. Now it seemed he had his hands full with death and vicious assault. First the Floyd girls, then Miller; now this extremely attractive young woman. It was just as well, perhaps, for Dr Misso's peace of mind that he was not at the time aware of the body found in the sea.

"She'll be all right in the morning, after a good sleep," he said, his spectacles glinting in the light. "She's had a heavy blow on the shoulder, but no bones broken, fortunately. It's her leg that is the main trouble. I've cleaned and dressed it, but the important thing is for her to rest." He looked at Blake significantly, then snapped shut the catches of the black leather bag against the divan. He straightened himself up, his heavily starched white drill suit crackling. "I've left a sedative for her."

He held out his hand to Blake, looking with professional interest at the scratches and bruises on his body. It was obvious that Blake himself was not in the least concerned about them. It wasn't surprising, thought Dr Misso. He had heard of Sexton Blake.

"I'm honoured to meet you, sir," he said. "I only wish it had been under happier circumstances."

Blake shook the little doctor's hand and thanked him for his assistance. Dr Misso left, heading homewards, and Blake turned back to find Paula watching him.

"He's gone, hasn't he, chief?" she asked, levering herself up on one elbow. "I'm all right, honestly I am. Sorry I messed things up."

Blake pushed her gently back onto the cushions. "You can tell me what you want to tell me lying down," he said.

Paula told him what had happened. Blake listened in silence, then he said: "I suppose you didn't get a glimpse of your attacker—anything which might give us a clue?"

"No, chief. All I saw was this dark form. He had the bar raised for another blow when the taxi must have frightened him off—"

"The bar? An iron bar, do you mean?" asked Blake.

She shuddered. "That was the impression I got. Then I must have passed out. I don't remember anything more until I came round here."

Blake's face was grim. "I think we can safely assume that your attacker was the same person who killed Miller and the two Floyd girls. You had a very lucky escape, Paula."

"Don't I know it!" Then she looked at Blake, her face a little crestfallen. "I haven't been able to get through to the police yet—"

"That can wait," said Blake. "The body can't run away."

Mary Floyd gasped. "Body? What body? Not another one?" All the colour had drained from her cheeks.

In a few brief words Blake described his finding of the body in the sea, and of the attack upon him.

"We've both had very fortunate escapes," he said. His eyes held a hard, bleak look. He realised just how lucky Paula had been. She had escaped death by seconds only.

Well, it was Round One to the unknown. Now he would start squaring accounts.

He looked at Mary Floyd, now seated limply in a chair. "I think you should try to get some rest, Mrs Floyd. And don't worry about your husband. He appears to be a very determined man—I'm sure he'll be all right." Inwardly he did not feel so sure, but there was no point in alarming her further.

"You said something . . . about a body," she muttered.

"In the sea, tangled in some netting. Probably an unfortunate fisherman," he said soothingly. "Please don't think any more about it. We shall probably know more in the morning."

She nodded goodnight and went wearily upstairs, her figure drooping. Blake waited until he heard her bedroom door close, then turned to Melder.

"Phone the police, Richard," he said tautly. "Get Vandebona if possible. I think we've found Eddie Vance!"

CHAPTER XV

The Spider is too Fly

Life hath quicksands, life hath snares.
Longfellow: *Maidenhood.*

FREDDIE DE SOYSA gave a sigh of relief as he heard the outer door open and close. He was seated in the lounge of the house he had entered, in the dark. He had been waiting for some time but he had been glad of the chance to relax. It was a welcome change from the scratchy, cold embrace of the hedge in which he had been crouched in acute discomfort for the past few hours.

He heard the door being locked and the sharp click as the light was switched on. Then came a startled exclamation:

"What are you doing here? Who are you?"

Freddie rose, grinning. He gave an exaggerated bow.

"My name is immaterial. The point is, I know you."

"Well, I don't receive callers at this hour—especially strangers. You had better get out at once before I call the police."

Freddie shook his head. "Surely it isn't a crime to pay a social call?"

"The only call you'll be having is from the police, as I just said, if you don't get out."

"I think," said Freddie, grinning more widely than ever, "that you are going to have second thoughts about that. Unless, of course, you'd like the cops to call for *you*—with handcuffs."

"What do you mean?"

"Exactly what I said," smiled Freddie. He was feeling on top of the world. This was his moment of triumph. He had beaten everybody, including the famous Sexton Blake. He was in line for that thirty thousand rupees reward. But he might get more if he played his cards right; enough perhaps to set him up for the rest of his life.

"I said I know you," he said. "That's because I saw your name on the gate. Such a respectable name, too. Who would ever dream you were a killer?"

"You must be out of your mind! Leave this house at once!"

Freddie sank back into the chair.

"Let's be seated, shall we? And don't try to pretend—not with me. You see, I've been watching you for some time." This wasn't true, but it would help him to tighten the screws. "I saw you come out of this house and go into the one adjoining that of the Floyds; you were so obviously up to no good that I simply had to follow you. I watched through the window . . . When you'd finished you left in a hurry and as you were about to re-enter your own house, you saw Miss Dane limping up the lane. You hid in the hedge until she got close, then attacked her. You'd have killed her if that taxi hadn't arrived when it did—"

Freddie paused. "How am I doing so far? I'd beat Blake at his own game, wouldn't I? Let's go on, shall we? You didn't return here at once; you went towards the beach and I lost sight of you. But I knew you'd be back, so I decided to wait for you here. It was obliging of you to leave the door unlocked—"

He pulled out a crumpled packet of cheap cigarettes from his shirt pocket. "Do you mind if I smoke?" He lit up, settled himself more comfortably and blew out a stream of smoke. "When you went into that house next to Floyds' you were carrying an iron bar—the same bar you attacked Miss Dane with. I've no doubt at all that it's what you used to kill the Floyd girl with, the older one. What the police would call 'the murder weapon', in fact."

"I don't know what you're talking about! You're out of your mind! Get out!"

Freddie was enjoying himself. "Don't take that tone with me! The police would be highly interested in meeting you—so would Blake, I've no doubt. I have only to tell them what I saw—and they'll put their own construction on it. Also I shall collect a reward of thirty thousand rupees. But I've decided to give you a chance. After all, the deaths of those silly girls means nothing to me. Supposing I decide to keep quiet? Would you care to show your gratitude in a tangible form? Say fifty thousand rupees?" Freddie's mind added: "to start with", but he did not speak it. "After all, what is fifty thousand if you escape the gallows?"

"But I've not got that much money!"

"Ah, that's better! You're beginning to sound ... reasonable. It's no use pretending, is it? This is strictly between you and me, and if you want it to stay that way you'd better find the cash. Finding it is your funeral—either way. I'll give you twenty-four hours. If you don't—er—honour your obligations by then I shall go straight to the police. I shall want the money in cash, in small notes—fives and tens. I'll let you know later about the time and place."

"How do I know you'll keep your word? How do I know you won't ask for more?"

"You'll have to take the word of a gentleman." Freddie rose to his feet, drawing himself up to his full height of five feet six inches. "As I said, I'll keep in touch. And don't try double-crossing me or it will be the worse for you!"

"But what about your friends? How do I know they won't go to the police?"

"What friends? I have no—" Freddie stopped abruptly, cursing himself. He had been taken off-guard. "I have no such friends," he amended. "They will do as I say. Incidentally, one of them knows I am here," he added.

"How?"

Freddie forced a laugh; he was beginning to sweat, wishing he had taken some kind of precaution before entering the house. He went on: "I told my friend I proposed to do a little—private investigating. He knew I was suspicious of a certain somebody in Lotus Lane—yourself. If I don't return safely he will know that something has happened to me—and who is responsible."

The other did not reply, then gave a nod. Freddie breathed again. He had thought at first that the murderer would guess that he was lying.

Freddie's companion looked at the cigarette dangling from between his lips, and held out a slightly trembling hand. "I think . . . May I have one of your cigarettes?"

"Sure. But no tricks, mind. I've got a gun." Freddie wished he had. His only weapons were the cosh and a penknife with a two-inch blade which he had bought because of its corkscrew attachment. He had full confidence, however, that he could handle the situation.

He threw the packet of cigarettes and a box of matches.

"Catch!"

He wasn't going to let the killer get too close to him.

The matchbox fell to the carpet and the other stooped to pick it up.

Then Freddie found himself falling in a wild flurry of arms and legs as the carpet was suddenly pulled away from beneath him. He saw the killer leap forward, saw the iron bar appear from a concealed pocket, saw it rise and fall in the clenched hand.

Then it hit his head with stunning force and he saw nothing more.

Sexton Blake did not wait for the police to arrive. He left Melder to deal with them. Melder would take them to where the body lay, following Blake's explicit instructions.

He himself had other work to do. Urgent work. He had delayed only long enough to have a quick shower and change into shirt and slacks. Paula was in bed and now Blake was walking up the short drive of the house next door.

The light was on in the lounge. It hand't been there earlier in the evening. Allen's Anglia was under the porch.

He thumbed the bell-push. He heard the bell ringing somewhere within the house.

He kept on ringing, but there was no response.

Blake frowned. Was Allen such a heavy sleeper that he had not heard the bell? Or had he heard it and was afraid to answer it? Or had something happened to him?

Blake gave a final unproductive ring, then walked to the french windows of the study.

He opened his penknife, selected one of its blades of finely-tempered steel. It would have taken him only a few seconds to slip back the catch of one of the windows.

Then he felt a faint tingle of premonition creep down his spine.

It wasn't necessary to force open the window. It opened to his touch.

Blake paused. Perhaps Allen had forgotten to close the windows. But it seemed unlikely. From what he had heard of him, Allen appeared to be a careful man of fixed habits. Certainly he would not have made things easy for a burglar.

Blake heard a car snarling on gear down the lane, its head-lights blazing. On the hood of the car was the illuminated sign: "POLICE". Behind it came a van. Both vehicles drew up at the gate of Floyd's house. The police had come pretty quickly, he thought.

He turned to the window, swung it cautiously outwards. The well-oiled hinges were testimony to Allen's methodical nature.

Somewhere in the vicinity a killer was on the prowl. The killer had tried to get him and Paula, and had failed. At that time both he and Paula had been taken unawares, and both had been unarmed. But now it was different. Before leaving Blake had armed himself with his Luger.

He pulled the gun from his hip pocket and thumbed back the safety catch. With the weapon ready in his right hand he pushed the heavy curtain aside with the other, inch by inch. He kept well away from the window, so as not to silhouette himself against the starlight.

He waited, tensed.

Nothing happened.

He thrust a leg inside. Then, with his gun at the ready, he

leapt forward, and as he did so he let the curtain fall back.

Still nothing.

He took a step forward in the darkness and his foot encountered something soft.

He bent down quickly. His exploring hand told him that there was a body on the floor.

Blake switched on the slim torch he had brought with him.

The pencil-thin beam fell on an outstretched hand on which he had inadvertently trodden. He let the light traverse back and forth, showing him the inanimate man on the carpet.

He straightened, then went across to the door and flooded the room with light. Pocketing the gun he raised the fallen man easily and set him down on the divan. The man was corpulent, with sandy hair and sallow features; on his forehead was a contused bump.

Blake found a bottle of brandy on the sideboard. He poured some into a glass, raised the man's head and got a little of the spirit between his lips. The man spluttered and threshed about with his arms and legs. Blake had to hold him to prevent him from falling off the divan.

"That's better," he said.

The man's eyes opened and he stared around him uncomprehendingly. "Wh-where am I?" he asked. His voice was little more than a croak.

"Right in your own house, Mr Allen."

"And who are you?"

"My name is Blake. Sexton Blake."

"Sexton Blake!" The man jerked bolt upright. "Ugh! My head!" He raised a hand gingerly, felt the bump, and winced. But his eyes were alert now and colour had returned to his cheeks. He made as though to get up, but Blake gently pushed him back.

"Take it easy; you've had a nasty crack. I'm sorry I had to call on you at this hour of the night—or rather, morning—but it would seem lucky for you that I did. I found the window open and you lying on the floor. What happened?"

"I—I don't know." Allen rested his head between his hands. "Heston told me you'd be coming to Floyd's place to look into these hellish murders. I wanted to meet you last night, after I returned from Galle—then this happened. Anyway, I'm glad to meet you now, Mr Blake." He gave a shaky smile. "Can I get you anything to drink?"

"No, thanks all the same. But if you could tell me—"

"I'm sorry, Mr Blake. You see, it's like this—I have to go to Galle once a week. That's where our main sub-station in the south is. I'm the accountant and I have to check up on the books there. Last evening, as usual, I left the Fort office at five. I didn't come here but drove straight down to Galle. Usually my work takes me only a couple of hours. I stay overnight at the rest-house, and return home by noon the following day. But yesterday I wanted to get back before midnight because I was expecting a call around one o'clock, when reception would be clear."

He paused. "I must explain that I am a radio enthusiast, and have my own transmitter and receiver. The call I was expecting was from a friend up-country who, like myself, is a 'radio ham' as we're called—"

Blake nodded. "All right. Go on."

"I drove in here about ten-thirty," Allen resumed. "I let myself in through the front door. It was locked—just as I'd left it. I went straight across the lounge. My apparatus is on the ground floor in what was originally the pantry. Then I thought I heard a noise from this room. I had switched on the lights of the lounge, of course. I could see the curtains leading to the lounge swaying, as if in a draught. I thought I might have forgotten to close one of the windows of the study, so I came in. I felt for the switch—and then it happened. Something struck me on the head and I felt myself falling. That's all I can remember until I opened my eyes just now and saw you." Sudden fears showed in Allen's eyes. "My God, I wonder if he's stolen anything!"

He jumped up from the divan and stumbled from the study before Blake could stop him. He went through every room, with Blake at his heels. Nothing had apparently been disturbed. And nothing was missing.

"Well, I'm glad you turned up when you did," said Allen finally, on a note of relief. "You evidently surprised the burglar."

Blake said nothing. Whoever had entered Allen's house had been no burglar. There had been no sign of an intruder when he arrived which, according to Allen's account, must have been some time after Allen had been struck down. If the intruder had been a thief he would have had ample time to get away with whatever he wanted.

But nothing had been taken. Who, then, was the mysterious intruder and what had been his purpose in entering the house?

They had ended their search upstairs, in the lounge and in the study. Blake had found in the lounge something of significance—the marks of gum on the otherwise neatly-kept table and a book set in large type which had been thrust the wrong way round into the low bookshelf. A number of letters had been cut from the pages.

Now they were in the short passage that led from the rear of the lounge. There were three doors. "The kitchen and bathroom are at the end," explained Allen. He opened the nearest door and turned to Blake. "My transmitter's here," he said on a note of pride.

He switched on the light and a cry of horror broke from him. He pointed a quivering finger.

"My God! Look!" he cried.

Scattered over the room was the wreckage of electronic equipment; smashed tubes and condensers, bits of fine wire and chips of bakelite covering. Somebody had systematically destroyed every bit of Allen's transmitter.

Like a man demented he crawled amongst the debris, heedless of the pieces of broken glass.

"Gone!" he moaned. "All gone! Smashed, ruined, done for." His anguish was pitiful to see. He was in tears as he picked up each useless piece and dropped it again.

"There's nothing left. By God, if I find out who's done this, I'll kill him! I'll tear him apart with my bare hands—"

His voice rose shrilly. Blake, gently but firmly, helped him to his feet.

"There's nothing that can be done here. Pull yourself together, man!" He half-dragged the whimpering Allen back to the study. He poured out a stiff drink of brandy and held it towards him. "Here—take this!"

By sheer strength of personality he forced Allen to calm down. Then he questioned him—right from the beginning, from the time of Angela Floyd's death.

But there was nothing the accountant could add to what Blake had already learned from the police reports. Allen could still not explain away the empty petrol tank.

"I knew there was very little petrol left," he said. "But that didn't worry me. It was enough to get me to the filling station at the junction. I have often done it. Anyway, the tank wasn't bone dry when I got it started. It wouldn't have started at all if it had been, would it?"

Blake nodded. "And you didn't see or hear anyone going into Floyd's house?"

Allen shuddered. He had recourse to the brandy again. "All I saw and heard were the crows—apart from hearing Mary chase Judy off to school and seeing her and Jeff leave. Conrad Miller and Eva left shortly afterwards."

He was as equally baffled over the whole affair as everyone else appeared to be.

Blake asked: "How long were you in Floyd's house, after you had discovered Angela?"

"About half an hour, until Dr Misso came. I phoned him first, though of course there was nothing he could do for that poor girl. Then I rang up on the direct line. I thought I could get Eva to tell Jeff and Mary that there had been an accident. I knew Heston had left for Galle, but he answered the phone. Then I contacted the police. It took me at least thirty minutes."

"Who was the first to come?"

"Why, Dr Misso. He lives close by. Then the police—the Kollupitiya police station is also close by, just past the filling station. The others came shortly afterwards. I know, of course, that the police suspect me—but I swear I had nothing to do with these ghastly crimes—"

"The police suspect everybody; it's their duty to do so," said Blake soothingly. "But we shall catch the murderer in the end, you may be certain of that." He glanced at his watch. It was three o'clock in the morning. He rose.

"But my transmitter!" wailed Allen. "My equipment! Can't you help me to find out who is responsible for—"

He broke off as the door bell rang.

"Who can that be?" he muttered uneasily. He looked at Blake. "You don't think—" He did not finish but clearly the thought of the unknown killer was in his mind.

"We'll find out," said Blake briefly. He had his Luger ready. "Open the door on the latch—and keep right behind it."

Allen obeyed, trembling.

"Who is it?" he asked, through the opening.

"Police here, sir," said a voice which Blake recognised as Vandebona's. "I'm sorry to disturb you, but could you please come with us?" Vandebona caught sight of Blake. "We found the body, Mr Blake. It's in the van outside. We would like Mr Allen to identify it."

Allen looked sick. "*Another* body?" he gasped. "Oh, my God!" Then he turned on Vandebona angrily, almost petulantly: "Why do you have to keep asking *me* to make these identifications? This will be the fourth time—Really, Inspector, isn't there anybody else who can—"

"I'm sorry, sir," said Vandebona stolidly. "We can't very well ask any of the ladies."

Allen downed the rest of the brandy in one gulp.

The corpse lay on the floor of the police van—bloated, obscene, still in its shroud of wire mesh.

A police sergeant flashed a powerful torch on to it and on the thick ropes which had been used to haul it up from the sea.

Allen gulped and went a peculiarly green colour. The corpse's head was towards the rear doors.

"Well?" Behind him, Vandebona couldn't conceal his impatience. "Well?" he demanded again, when no reply was forthcoming from Allen.

Allen let out a long-held breath.

"It's him," he said. "Eddie. Eddie Vance. Excuse me . . ."

He tottered away quickly. He hadn't time to reach the hedge. He was sick for two or three minutes.

Sexton Blake stepped out from where he had been standing in the shadows. He took the torch from the sergeant. Followed by the CID man he climbed into the van and examined the body.

The effects of the long immersion in the sea were only too plainly visible. Putrefying flesh had swelled through the mesh. Fishes had attacked parts of the body. The eyes were mere gaping sockets.

Blake gently turned the body over. The back of the skull had been battered in. Blake was reminded of the blows that had smashed the life out of Angela Floyd, and the blow that had felled Paula. The same murder weapon, he felt certain.

His eyes were steely as he backed out of the van and handed the torch back to the sergeant.

"All right," he told Vandebona. "I've finished now. Thanks."

The sergeant locked the door and got into the front of the van. Vandebona spoke to the driver.

"Get going, Idroos. Take the body to the morgue. I'll be along."

The van sped up the lane. Vandebona said: "Well, that's that. The fourth victim . . ."

Blake nodded. "Yes," he said tonelessly. "The fourth body. But it was actually the first."

Would there be more? And how many?

CHAPTER XVI

Web of Horror

Prison'd in a parlour, snug and small,
Like bottled wasps upon a southern wall.
William Cowper: *Retirement.*

"Damn!" snarled Jeffrey Floyd. "Damn and blast it!"

He expressed other sentiments as well, all of them unprintable. But there was no fear of anybody hearing them. Nobody could, even if they had tried, because he couldn't say the words aloud. They were muffled by a gag.

The gag consisted of a wad of foul-smelling cloth held in place by an even worse smelling silk scarf tied securely at the back of his head.

The gag, however, was the least of his discomforts. He would not have minded being deprived of the power of making himself audible if only he could have moved his limbs freely. But he could not, because his arms and legs were bound. They were bound even more tightly by someone who had evidently taken a sadistic pleasure in making them bite into his flesh.

Floyd had lost count of how long he had been in that condition. All he knew, with growing alarm, was that if he was to continue to remain so for any further length of time his blood circulation would be totally impeded. Already his extremities were beginning to feel benumbed.

It was poor consolation that he now knew who the killer was. It was the crowning irony!

He mentally kicked himself. A hell of a fine mess he had made of things, thinking he could outsmart Sexton Blake and track down the murderer of Angela and Judy on his own.

All he had done was walk straight into the killer's hands.

For the killer was somebody he had least suspected.

Throughout he had felt certain that the murderer was somebody who lived in the lane; somebody who had been able to watch the comings and goings of his family; perhaps knowing them intimately. And he had his suspicions. As yet they were still indefinite and undefinable, but he felt sure that if he could find somewhere close at hand, where he could watch and wait, he would stumble upon the proof he needed. He could not go home; there were too many pressures, too much coming and going of the police. Also, Sexton Blake was there. He had to be somewhere unsuspected.

And finally he had hit upon the perfect answer. He had smiled to himself with relief when it came to him.

He had abandoned Melder's car near the British High Commission office, jumped into the first bus going towards the Fort, and taken a room at a small hotel, registering under an assumed name. He had intended to make his way to the lane after a short rest and a bath but tiredness had overwhelmed him and he had fallen asleep, waking up shortly after four-thirty. He had made his telephone call at five o'clock, apologising to the person at the other end of the line for the inconvenience, stressing the urgency of his plan.

It was still dark when he reached the lane and entered the house of his benefactor. He had been warmly welcomed, his apologies brushed aside.

"Of course we must all do everything we can to help trap the murderer. You are welcome to stay here as long as you like. But you must be tired and hungry still—would you like something to eat?"

"No, thank you." He had waved the offer aside.

"Some brandy, then?"

This he had accepted with gratitude. He had poured himself a generous measure and tossed it off, feeling it glow within him, spreading its optimistic warmth.

The glow hadn't lasted long. Suddenly the room seemed to be spinning around him, like a gigantic catherine wheel. That had been his last impression—that, and the sound of soft, mocking laughter—before darkness overwhelmed him.

When he opened his eyes again it was in blackness as profound as the pit from which he had returned. His head was aching abominably and it took him some time to remember where he was—and to realise what had happened to him.

When he knew, he groaned inwardly. Instead of trapping the killer, he had played directly into his captor's hands! He was a prisoner; trussed up and dumped in this dark hole. He wondered why he had not been killed at once; had the murderer some other plan in mind?

If only he had done as Sexton Blake had said! All he could hope now was that Mary was safe.

There was no use in crying over spilt milk. At least he knew now who the murderer was—the killer of his two daughters. And he was still alive; it might still be possible to escape and bring the murderer to justice.

Floyd set about trying to loosen his bonds. He rolled about, straining every nerve, gritting his teeth as pain shot through his cramped limbs, trying to get his fingers into one of the knots that held his wrists together. He knew it was a near-impossible task, but he kept on trying. He rolled sideways. He moved by slow, agonising degrees. If he could find something against which he could rub the ropes so that they became frayed and loosened and snapped!

But that kind of thing happened only in books or films. Even Houdini could not have got out of this one!

He was almost suffocated by the gag, and the blood was pounding in his ears. He knew he could not hold out much longer. He made a final despairing effort.

Then he felt a shock wave of sheer horror engulf him.

In the darkness, cold fingers closed around his wrist.

CHAPTER XVII

Tangle with the Threads

O, what a tangled web we weave,
When first we practice to deceive.
Sir Walter Scott: *Marmion.*

"Now," said Sexton Blake. "Let's go through what we've managed to find out so far. It should help clarify things a little."

Before leaving for his own house, Allen had given him an additional item of information. The wire which had been meshed around the body was his. He had bought it on Friday evening and left it in the rear of his car. In the excitement of the subsequent happenings he had quite forgotten about it.

"That's his story," the sceptical Vandebona told Blake grimly. "He's chosen a convenient time to remember it!"

Blake nodded. He was thinking that Allen was in a very tight spot. "He'd know, of course, that now it's been found—and around a corpse—it could be traced back to him." But why the attack on Allen in his own house, and the destruction of the radio transmitter? Blake felt sure these had not been faked.

He had gone with Vandebona to Eva Miller's house; she had to be informed of Eddie's death. It was a task neither of them relished, and they had been relieved to find that she wasn't in, even though they knew the unhappy moment had merely been postponed.

After a brief conference Vandebona had left, requesting

Blake to call with Paula at nine in the morning for the inquest proceedings on Eddie Vance. Blake had then returned to the Floyd house.

Paula and Mary Floyd were sleeping. Melder was still in the lounge, smoking innumerable cigarettes and keeping watch with Paula's Beretta in his hand.

Blake had told him to get some sleep, had commandeered the rest of the coffee in the big flask which Mary had provided, and had retired to the study. There he had quietly reviewed the case.

He had then snatched a few hours' sleep and when Paula woke he was already up, bathed and shaved and showing no signs of the strain of the previous night. Paula was limping and moved her shoulder stiffly, but she put a brave face on her injuries.

Melder had left after breakfast, and Vandebona had telephoned to say that the Humber had been found and Melder had gone to collect it from the nearby police station, which was almost opposite the entrance to the British High Commission, where Floyd had abandoned the car.

Now Blake was in the study with Paula. They had returned from the inquest on Eddie Vance, and fortified themselves with a strong brandy apiece.

Blake reached into the breast pocket of his coat, which he had hung on the back of his chair, and produced the neatly-written notes he had made the previous night.

"Let's go through these, Paula," he said. He added: "It will take some time. Better make yourself comfortable."

"I'm all right," said Paula. She was leaning back in a deep leather armchair, her long nyloned legs crossed, the bandage around her injured ankle showing through the delicate mesh.

Blake handed the sheaf of notes to her. "On second thoughts, you read them out to me."

Paula brought her chair closer. Blake leaned back, his legs thrust out under the desk, his eyes closed and his supple fingers forming a pyramid on his chest. He looked completely relaxed, but Paula knew that her chief's mind was as alert as ever.

She began to read from the notes, with growing interest and surprise.

Blake had made out a time-table of events, with queries interpolated.

Saturday

1 a.m.   Eddie Vance gets a phone call (not yet traced) according to the evidence of Conrad Miller, and leaves the house. Not seen again until last night, when his body was found in the sea. All have alibis for the time of leaving except Heston and Allen, who were alone. Others alibi one another.

10.25 a.m.   Judy Floyd leaves classroom, ostensibly to go to the lavatory. Evidence that this had become a regular occurrence with her, dating back to about a fortnight earlier.

10.27 a.m.   Emily Syms retires to her office on ground floor. Says she has a bad headache.

10.40 a.m.   Angela Floyd's body found by Allen.

Queries:

1. What happened in the past fortnight to make Judy leave the classroom at 10.25 every day?

2. Did Emily Syms really have a headache? If so, what was the cause of same? She has no alibi.

3. Why was Allen's petrol tank dry? Was the "break-down" a cover for staying behind to make advances to Angela?

4. Is Bella Syms really deaf? Even if she is, she is not blind. Did she see something and is afraid to tell? She has no alibi.

5. Is Houston's story of forgotten papers a cover-up for murder? He says he can't place exactly when he turned back. According to Vandebona, police checks so far have drawn a blank. No alibi.

6. WHY was Angela killed?

7. Was the murder premeditated? The murder weapon has not been found but indication is that murderer had it when entering Floyd house.

Notes:

(a) Eva Miller's alibi is weak.

(b) Conrad Miller's alibi checked and found true. He was at the bar, up to the time of the murder.

Now for the events of the night (went on Blake's notes):

8 to 9 p.m.   Vandebona at Miller's house. Ample time for anyone to tamper with Miller's car.

10 p.m. (approx.)   Miller's death in car crash. Murder by remote control. Nobody has an alibi.

Queries:

8. Was an outsider responsible? A business rival or firm?

9. If both murders (Angela's and Miller's) were not "business" killings, did murderer think Miller had some knowledge, real or imaginary, about Angela's death? *Why* was Miller killed?

Sunday

Midnight (approx.)   Judy leaves home. Evidence that she left of own accord, taking torch and air gun and wearing dark clothes.

Monday

12.32 a.m. (approx.)   Train runs over Judy's body. She has been strangled. Heston, Allen and Mrs Miller have no alibis. Syms sisters and Floyds alibi each other.

Queries:

10. What knowledge did Judy have that made her dangerous to the killer? Where, how and when did she acquire it?

10 p.m. (approx.)   Finding of Eddie's body.

10.30 p.m.   Attack on Allen and destruction of his transmitter.

10.45 p.m. (approx.)   Attack on Paula.

11.15 p.m. (approx.)   Attack on self.

Queries:

11. Who was Eddie Vance's caller?

12. Why was he killed?

13. Why was Allen's transmitter smashed?

Paula looked up. "Thirteen questions," she said slowly.

"And I don't see any clue to the answers. This case *is* tough!"

Sexton Blake opened his eyes and straightened himself up in his chair.

"Nevertheless, the answers are there—somewhere," he replied sombrely. He reached for his cigarettes and offered one to Paula. They lit up and Blake went on: "And there are a few more questions, too—for example, where has Floyd gone? Whatever his plans were, it is inconceivable that he should not have got in touch with his wife, knowing the state of mind she is in. Has anything happened to him, I wonder?"

Paula looked unhappy. "That poor woman! What she has been through! If anything *has* happened to her husband—" She did not finish but her expression was eloquent.

Blake went on: "There is one question that doesn't fit into the general scheme at all. Have you spotted it?"

She looked at the notes again. "You mean the smashing of the transmitter?"

"Yes. There seems to have been some connection between the other happenings. They form part of the pattern of murder. But this seems to be completely out of place. It appears to be senseless—but there must be some very good reason for it. If we can find out what that reason is, I think we shall be on the way towards getting the answers to the other questions. It may provide the vital clue to the identity of the killer."

He went on, quietly: "Let's theorise, Paula. First, take Heston. He was at home the night Eddie was murdered. Supposing it was he who rang Eddie, met him outside Miller's house, killed him and took him away in Allen's car. Perhaps he proposed leaving the body on the railway tracks, to be run over by a train. But seeing the wire mesh in the car gave him another idea. So he rolled the body up in it and dropped it into the sea. Then he returned Allen's car and walked back home. He didn't know that he had used up practically every drop of petrol in the tank.

"The following day—Sunday—he set out for Galle but turned back for those "missing papers". He knew Angela would be alone. He drove home, walked to Floyd's house.

Allen's presence next door, tinkering with his car, must have given him a jolt. But Allen was too engrossed to notice him. Heston let himself in, made advances to Angela, and killed her when she repulsed him.

"He then came downstairs, wondering how to get out of the house unseen. His clothes would be bloodstained; he would have to change them. He went out through the rear door and made his way back to his own place along the backs of the houses. By this time Allen had seen the crows and was already running towards the Floyd's house. It was easy enough for Heston to change into fresh clothes, hide or destroy the others, and drive back to his office, in time to get Allen's call."

Blake paused. "Next, we come to Miller's murder. Heston was at home that evening. He feared Miller had something on him. It would have been a simple matter for him to have arranged that death trap in the car. As for Judy, there is no doubt that she knew who the killer was. She tried a spot of blackmail—and paid for it with her life. Heston was at home that night, too."

"It fits," said Paula cryptically. "Perhaps too well. But why would Heston kill Eddie?"

"It's obvious that Eddie and Angela were having an affair. Jealousy can do strange things to a man's mind."

"Then you think it *was* Heston, after all?"

"That's how it could appear," said Blake. "But substitute Allen for Heston, and you have an equally strong case against Allen. Don't forget he had that roll of wire mesh conveniently in his car. Like Heston, he must have known what was going on between Angela and Eddie."

He stubbed out the last of his cigarette and went on: "There's something else. In spite of what Miller said about he and Eddie getting on together, that wasn't strictly true. They quarrelled quite a lot. Don't forget Eddie was his stepson, not his son. And Miller also had a roving eye for the ladies. He could have had a crush on Angela *and* known about her and Eddie. He was in the house when Eddie received that telephone call which took him out—he could have followed him thinking he was going on a secret assignation with Angela. Perhaps they quarrelled—and in the heat of the moment Miller killed Eddie.

"Until now we've all assumed that the murders were committed by the same person. But supposing there are two murderers? It's inconceivable that Eva Miller should kill her own son—but she could have killed Angela. She was passionately devoted to Eddie and could have been intensely jealous—and furious—at what was going on between him and Angela. She might even have suspected that her husband was attracted towards the girl, which would have given her an added incentive to get rid of her."

"But she was in the office at the time Angela was killed," Paula pointed out.

"Quite right, Paula. But she knew Heston had left for Galle and wasn't due back until evening. Floyd and his wife were busy in their section of the office, and Miller had gone out. In any case, her services wouldn't be required by them. She knew she wouldn't be interrupted. So she walked out through Heston's private door and drove down here. She would have taken a taxi to the top of the lane, walked down to Floyd's house, seen Angela, quarrelled with her and killed her. Then, like Heston, she could have left the house by the rear door and got back to her own place to change her clothes—"

"But wouldn't somebody have noticed it, at the office?"

"The change of clothing? Not if she was careful to choose something similar."

"But why would she kill Conrad Miller—her husband?"

"Perhaps also because of Angela, although I'm not too happy about that explanation of it. On the other hand, she might have had a quarrel with him afterwards and tinkered with the car in a moment of fury. However, as I've just said, I'm not satisfied with this probability."

"And Judy?"

"As I've already said, I think she witnessed the killing of her sister and had to be silenced on that count. In fact, her death appears to be the only one with any real motive behind it."

"That makes three suspects," said Paula. "Heston, Allen and Eva Miller. And Conrad Miller could have killed Angela. On the other hand, he was already dead when Judy was killed, which would seem to indicate that he was *not* Angela's murderer."

"Oh dear," sighed Paula. "The more we look at things, the more complicated they become."

"And you can add two more suspects, for the record," said Blake. "The Syms sisters. Either of them could have killed Angela—they had the opportunity, though I can't think of any possible motive. And neither of them has an alibi. Again, assuming the murders are all tied in together, I fail to see how —or why—Emily or Bella should have killed Eddie Vance or Conrad Miller."

Blake rose, took the sheaf of notes from Paula and thrust them, neatly folded, into the breast pocket of his light shark-skin suit.

"So much for the theorising," he said. "Now let's get the answers to some of the questions. I'd like to question Mrs Miller and Heston. Melder is due back here at any moment— leave him in charge and call in on the Syms sisters if I'm not back by then. Question them tactfully—particularly try to find out if Bella *did* hear or see anything that morning. You can wait here for me if you like. I'll drop in on my way back—"

He broke off as a knock sounded on the door. "Come in! Yes, what is it, Mrs Floyd?"

Mary Floyd came into the room hesitantly, closing the door behind her.

"I'm sorry to bother you, Mr Blake. I don't know if it's important or not, but it just struck me that Jeffrey's binoculars are still missing and—"

Blake's voice was sharp. "His binoculars? This is the first time they've been mentioned. What exactly do you mean by 'still missing'?"

"He missed them about two weeks ago. He was very annoyed about it; accused Judy of having taken them and perhaps lost them. But she denied it. He looked everywhere—we both did—but they haven't been found. I thought it might be important, though I can't see how . . ."

"Thank you, Mrs Floyd," said Blake. "It could be very important indeed. If you should remember anything else—anything at all, no matter how insignificant it seems—please let me know."

He held the door open for her and for Paula. Over Mary's head he and Paula exchanged glances.

Again that significant two weeks!

For the second time in the past few hours Blake rang the bell of Mrs Miller's house. He didn't have to turn away this time. Mrs Miller herself answered the door. Her face was pale and streaked and her eyes were red with weeping. He introduced himself.

"Please come in, Mr Blake," she said dully. "Bob—Mr Heston—told me about you."

"I'm sorry to intrude on your grief, Mrs Miller," Blake said, for it was obvious that she had been informed of Eddie's death. "If you should prefer that I call at some other time—"

"No, it's all right. Please come in." Her voice was still completely without expression; it was as though grief had drained all emotion from her. She added: "The police told me this morning about . . . Eddie."

"I am very, very sorry," said Blake again. There was nothing else he **could** say.

"You came here after—after they'd found him, didn't you? I'm sorry I didn't come down. I didn't realise at the time—"

Blake was surprised. "You mean you were here, in the house, when Inspector Vandebona and myself called?"

"Yes. I was in the bedroom. I'd taken some sleeping pills and I was very drowsy. I heard the knocking but didn't think it could be important. If I'd known . . ."

"It's all right," said Blake, wondering if she were telling the truth. There had been no light in the bedroom when he and the Inspector had called; in fact, there had been no indication at all that the house was occupied. Had she been in bed—or had she been out that night?

She went on: "Conrad's death . . . it has upset me very much, as you can imagine. And I was worried about Eddie. I had a terrible feeling that I would never see him again. And I was right, wasn't I?" She choked back a sob.

Blake nodded sympathetically. But in spite of her obviously genuine grief there was a peculiar evasiveness in her manner. Was she hiding something? Many things had happened last night—the attack on himself and on Paula; the attack on Allen and the destruction of his transmitter. Did Eva Miller know anything about these things?

But he allowed nothing of his thoughts to be reflected in his expression.

"If you could just answer a few questions for me . . ." he suggested quietly. "It could help, perhaps, to track down the killer of your husband, and of Eddie—"

She passed a hand across her forehead. "Anything you say, Mr Blake. But finding the killer won't bring Conrad and Eddie back, will it? What do you want to know?"

"Supposing we start with your first coming to this house, Mrs Miller?"

"Very well. Conrad and I arrived here from London with Mr Heston, the Floyds and Allen about two months ago. Mr Heston found jobs for myself and Mary. He didn't want any local staff handling top secret stuff, so he made me his confidential secretary. I had done a stenography course some time ago and all I needed was a little brushing-up. Mary was the receptionist and telephone operator. I liked the work—it took me out of the house and I've never been one for housework—but I wasn't really happy until Eddie joined us. We had left him in London, finishing a college course."

"When did Eddie join you?"

"About three weeks ago. He is . . . was . . . my only child." Her hands clenched and unclenched spasmodically. "My first husband, Clifford Vance, died in a car crash. That was in 1948 —Eddie was then two years old. The following year I met and married Conrad. He was then a junior partner of a big electrical firm in New York. I met him at a party in Manhattan.

"Conrad had worked for the Germans in Peenemunde. He came over to the States in 1946, soon after the war. He wasn't a Nazi; he was another of those scientists Hitler had roped in. Before he married me he had obtained naturalisation papers and changed his name—"

"Changed his name?" repeated Blake sharply.

"Yes. His real name was Konrad Muller. But before the war he had been about ten years in the States and had become quite Americanised. You would never have said he was a German.

"He quit his job after a few years and started out on his own. Then, by the time he had run through practically every cent we had—" She broke off and looked at Blake, almost apologetically "—He drank rather heavily at times, and he liked to treat his friends generously. Perhaps too generously."

"He had many friends?" asked Blake.

"Quite a number. A man never lacks friends while he can keep putting his hand into his pocket." Her voice was bitter.

"Did he have many women friends?" asked Blake. He added: "I'm sorry to have to ask you this, Mrs Miller, but it's important I should know everything."

For a moment he thought she did not intend to reply, then she nodded. "Yes. Conrad always had an eye for the women—especially young girls. We quarrelled frequently about it. But he was never really serious about any of them. He just liked to make a splash with them, show off, you know . . ."

He could have been serious about one—Angela Floyd, thought Blake. "Go on, please," he said gently.

"As I was saying—we were nearly broke when he met Floyd, who had come to attend a scientific convention. Floyd was interested in what Conrad was doing because he was working on the same lines. Jeffrey Floyd was with World Power and when he returned to London he fixed a top job with them for Conrad. So we quit Brooklyn—that's where we lived after we were married—and went to London."

"When was that?"

"In 1955. And that's where we've been for the past twelve years until Conrad's firm got this contract here. That's how we come to be in this awful place—" She dabbed at her eyes with a crumpled handkerchief.

Blake led her gently on to the events of the fateful Saturday.

"Did you notice anything out of the ordinary when you left the house, apart from Allen tinkering with his car?"

"No, nothing at all."

"And you drove straight to the office that day with your husband?"

"Yes. It's only a short distance. I was rather worried about Allen. He never turned up. Around ten forty-five I knew why —when he put through the call about Angela."

"And until that call came you were in the office?"

"Yes, Mr Blake. I didn't leave it, even for a moment. As the boss was away I busied myself spring-cleaning the files—it was a good opportunity, I thought. I don't go into the boss's room unless he rings for me. Normally he calls me in about eleven. That day he opened the communicating door and called me. I hadn't expected him to come back from Galle so soon. He told me that something had happened to Angela Floyd. Allen had rung up on the direct line to by-pass Mary at the switchboard."

"What time was that?"

"About 10.45."

"Was Mr Miller in then?"

"Yes. He was in the outer office. Mr Heston had informed them there—but he played it down because of Mary and Jeff. We came down to the house together."

Blake was watching her closely, without seeming to do so. Now he said: "Did you know that Eddie was friendly with Angela?" he asked.

"Yes." Her voice was non-committal.

"That he was, perhaps, more than . . . friendly?"

"Yes."

"What was your reaction, Mrs Miller?"

She looked at him squarely. "I wasn't very pleased. I didn't like Angela; I thought she was—fast. But I didn't think it was worth quarrelling with Eddie over. I knew it couldn't last; they don't, do they—affairs like that, I mean?"

"And your husband? What was his reaction?"

"He didn't seem interested. He and Eddie never had a great deal to say to each other, though they hit it off fairly well, I suppose."

"Now, about the previous night—or rather, early in the morning," went on Blake. "According to your husband, the call for Eddie came about one a.m. Did you hear it?"

"No. I didn't know about it until the morning, when Conrad told me at breakfast."

"You assumed it could have been Angela phoning him?"

"I suppose so. I wouldn't have put it past her." Again that trace of bitterness.

Blake was silent a moment, then he said: "The night your husband was killed. Did you notice anything suspicious that evening? Did you see or hear anyone outside?"

She shook her head, her face set in a frown of concentration.

"And the following night, when Judy Floyd was killed?"

She shook her head again. "I was in my room, sleeping. I sleep very heavily, once I've taken my pills."

Two dear old ladies, thought Paula. They actually wore lace, too—it was there in the collars and on the cuffs of their long cotton dresses. She wondered where the arsenic was. Even the old wooden chest was there, near the window, for the corpses. Then she chided herself for her fanciful thoughts; there was certainly nothing even remotely homicidal about her hostesses.

She was seated in the hot, furniture-packed hall of the Syms sisters' house. Through the gaping upholstery of the big sofa strands of coir fibre tickled and pricked her thighs. With difficulty she refrained from scratching herself; it would have seemed a doubly undignified gesture in front of these two extremely dignified old ladies.

The elder sister, Bella, sat on a high-backed chair, her

flowing skirts touching the ground, the cord of her hearing-aid running from a capacious pocket to her right ear. Emily was rocking gently in an ancient rocking-chair.

It was Emily who had admitted Paula when she pressed the yellowed bell-push. Her face had lightened with pleasure and she had been, as she excitedly expressed it, "all of a flutter" when Paula introduced herself. To think that the world-famous Sexton Blake was actually in residence across the road! And that his beautiful secretary should be visiting them!

"These dreadful murders!" she exclaimed as she ushered Paula into the hall. In her excitement she quite forgot her usual practice of locking the door and keeping the key. "Those two poor girls and that dear Mr Miller!" Paula noticed that she hadn't mentioned Eddie Vance and wondered if the omission had been accidental or deliberate.

"I can't sleep at night, wondering if we will all be murdered in our beds," Emily went on. "What with those noises in the attic and the rats running wild all over the ceiling!" She added: "But I must say I slept very well last night, though I do have that dreadful headache again. Just like I did on the day poor Angela—"

Her voice trailed away. "I must tell Bella you are here. Please sit down." She brushed the sofa with a thin hand. Paula held her breath and waited for the cloud of dust to subside.

"There! I won't be a moment." Emily bustled away in a flurry of skirts and apologies. Paula promptly seized her chance to examine the pictures on the wall and the miniature battlefield on the sideboard. Clearly the elder Syms sister had an obsession about the war. Well, some people were addicted to stamps and old coins. Why not miniatures of battle scenes? Still, it was an unusual hobby for a woman.

She went back to the sofa and settled herself as comfortably as possible as she heard footsteps on the stairs.

Bella entered the room slowly, followed by Emily. She greeted Paula warmly but Paula thought she saw the pale blue eyes flicker at the sight of her mini-skirt and the long graceful legs the skirt so generously exposed.

"Do sit down, Miss Dane," she said, for Paula had risen at her appearance. "I am sorry I kept you waiting. It's these dreadful stairs, you know. I can't imagine where I'd be without dear Emily to help me up and down."

Emily flushed. "It's nothing, Bella. Whatever I may do is small recompense for all that you have done for me."

Bella held up a large, queenly hand. "Not a word, Emily! You are my eyes and ears and hands, and you need not be ashamed of it. There, that's settled!"

She turned to Paula. Paula was staring at the carpet and wondering which of the splashes of red in its design could be blood. She gave herself a mental shake. She was, she thought, becoming altogether too fanciful.

She became conscious of the fact that the room was very warm—stifling in fact. None of the windows were open. How could they bear to live in such an atmosphere?

She was aware of Bella Syms addressing her.

"You look unwell, Miss Dane? Is it your leg?" She looked again at Paula's leg, with the bandage showing beneath the pale nylon stocking. "I hear that you were attacked last night, in the lane. Is there to be no end to these terrible happenings?"

Emily interposed. "Is this a social visit, Miss Dane, or have you come to ask us some questions?"

"Both," said Paula tactfully. "I've heard so much about you I felt I would like to pay you a visit. Also there is a slight possibility you might be able to tell me something which may help Mr Blake, and the police, in their inquiries. Often it is the smallest, most unimportant incident or detail which gives the clue to a crime—"

"Of course," said Bella. She rose from her chair. "But first let me make some coffee. Would you care for a cup, Miss Dane? You really do look very tired."

"Thank you," said Paula. "Iced?"

"Of course, if you wish." Bella moved towards the door, turning to smile back at her.

Here, thought Paula facetiously, comes the arsenic.

CHAPTER XVIII

Piece by Peace

For peace do not hope; to be just
you must break it.
  John Boyle O'Reilly: *Rules of the Road.*

HESTON'S HOUSE was about a hundred yards from Mrs Miller's, towards the top of the lane.

It seemed like a hundred miles to Sexton Blake as he walked up the slope, mopping his face with his handkerchief.

It was just past noon. The sun was directly overhead and the coconut trees and hedges afforded no cover.

On the main road ahead the heat haze shimmered over the tarmac. The sea was quiet and the sounds of traffic came clearly. From the rail tracks came the whistle of a steam locomotive.

Blake reached the gate, found it open and walked up the short drive. Heston's A55 was under the porch.

He rang the bell and was thankful that he did not have to wait for Heston opened the door instantly. He grinned when he saw Blake.

"Come in," he said. "What you need is a large iced beer."

"What I need are two large iced beers," said Blake.

Heston motioned Blake forward and closed the door after him. "You'll have to excuse my attire," he said. He was wearing a pair of white shorts and nothing else. Nevertheless, even with the air-conditioning, he was perspiring.

The lounge was quietly but expensively furnished. Blake

sank into a foam-rubber-cushioned chair. Heston went across to the refrigerator and came back with two bottles of Carlsberg, two large mugs and an opener. He put them down on a low table near Blake, opened the bottles and filled the mugs. He handed one to Blake.

"Cheers!" he said. He took a deep pull and smacked his lips appreciatively. "Cigarettes? Now we can talk. I heard about Eddie when I got back this morning. Bloody shame. That makes four murders—four in four days! It's incredible."

Blake put his glass down and blew a stream of smoke from his cigarette.

"Eddie's murder was the first," he said. "He was decoyed from his home by a phone call, obviously from somebody he knew—and trusted."

Heston shifted uneasily. "Eddie had a whole circle of friends—"

Blake cut across his words. "This belief that the murders are in some way connected with your firm—I think this is highly unlikely. I don't believe Big Business enters into it at all. We have to look elsewhere for the motive. It could be something personal." He paused a moment, then added: "The killer is somebody living here, in Lotus Lane."

Heston looked even more uncomfortable.

"One of us, eh?" he muttered. Beads of sweat glistened on his hairy chest. "That's not a very pleasant thought, is it. Any idea who it could be?"

"Not yet—but I intend to find out. Did you often visit Floyd's place?"

"Eh?" The question caught Heston unprepared—just as Blake had intended. "Why, yes—I mean, no. That is to say, I dropped in there of an evening for a chat sometimes. We all do. See here, what are you getting at?" His voice took on a truculent note.

Blake was unperturbed. "I'm not 'getting at' anything, in the sense you mean. Certainly nothing to be excited about. I merely want to get the whole thing clear in my mind. Don't take exception to any of my questions. Just answer them. After all, you're as anxious as the rest of us to see the murderer brought to justice, aren't you?"

"Of course," agreed Heston. He relaxed but his eyes were wary as he looked at Blake.

"I'll forestall you, Blake. If you think I had anything to do with Angela Floyd, forget it. She was a nice girl, but a bit too flighty for my liking. I didn't really take to her. I wouldn't say the same for Allen, though—he has a weakness for a pretty face." Heston took another pull at his mug. "So have I, come to that—but I prefer them rather more mature. You'll have to take my word for it, naturally."

"Naturally," Blake echoed. He stared back at Heston and Heston looked away. "Thank you for—as you have said—forestalling me. It's a pity, though, that you can't remember exactly where you turned back for those papers on that trip to Galle, the day Angela was killed."

"I was about to tell you that. As you may know, I went to Galle again yesterday, with Allen. That was our weekly trip. Allen came back early because he said he wanted to be with that infernal transmitter of his—By the way, I heard that somebody smashed it up. Pretty rotten and useless sort of thing to do, wasn't it?—I stayed overnight as usual and came back this morning. The point is, on the way back, it suddenly struck me just where I turned back that day. It was just past the level crossing where the road crosses the track for the first time and runs beside the sea. I looked at the name on the road signs. It's a place called Maggona."

"Have you told Vandebona?"

"First thing I did when I came back. He thanked me and said he'd check up."

"Fine." Vandebona had the resources to check up on the story. "Now, what's the distance to the place?"

"About forty miles. That makes eighty up and down. I left home shortly after nine. That doesn't give enough time, does it? For me to murder Angela, I mean. She was killed around ten-thirty. Besides, I turned into a filling station beyond Maggona on the way back and the man there remembers me.

I should think that lets me out." There was a faint grin of triumph on his face.

Does it? wondered Blake. He was thinking that it wouldn't be difficult to slip a hundred-rupee note into the hand of the man at the filling station in order that he could corroborate Heston's story.

He went on: "And when you returned to the office that day, were the others there?"

Heston looked surprised. "Sure. Except Allen, of course. I looked in on Jeff and Mary and asked about him. They told me about his car giving trouble. I was wondering why he was taking such a hell of a time fixing it when I got the call from him about Angela. It shook me, I don't mind telling you. I told Jeff and Mary—and Eva—that Angela had met with an accident. We locked up the office and came down."

"Now, about Eddie. Mrs Miller tells me that he came here from London about three weeks ago."

"That's right."

"And that Miller was his stepfather. Eddie's father, it seems, died in a car crash in 1948 and she married Miller the following year."

"Right again. I got all the dope on them from Jeff Floyd, who met Miller in the States and fixed him up with us. We made a very close security check on Miller because of his German origin. He had become an American citizen, but we weren't taking any chances. He was okay."

"Did Miller fight for the Germans?"

"Heck, no! He was one of the backroom boys—and one of the best. But he hated the Nazi set-up and the moment he got the chance he teamed up with the Yanks. That was in 1945, just before the push on Berlin."

"And where was he before that—during the war, I mean?"

"We compiled a complete dossier on him. He'd been in the Ruhr, Hamburg, Essen, Peenemunde and Berlin—always on top-drawer scientific work. Pity he never left Germany during the war. If he had come to Italy I might have met him there—like I met you."

There was silence for a while. The minds of both men travelled back over the years.

"That's where I first met the Syms sisters, too," resumed Heston, his voice taking on a reminiscent note. "You can't imagine what fine woman they were then! Emily was sixteen—a lovely, delicate girl. Bella was twenty—a strapping young creature, full of life. It was Emily who should have become the invalid."

He went on: "I met them near Naples. They were running a farm. They never had it so good as when the Allied troops came in and they were able to sell their produce at fancy prices. The Yanks, of course, beat us to the draw there." Heston's face had lit up; he was plainly living again those hectic days. "I remember it like yesterday. We were going along a narrow dusty village road some miles out of Naples when the engine of our jeep suddenly packed up. There were four of us, and I was the only officer. The other blokes are all dead now. We did our best to bring the jeep back to life, but we couldn't. We seemed to be bang in the middle of nowhere and we were hot and thirsty. Then a tractor came suddenly round a bend in the road, and a girl got out. She didn't say a word. She just looked in under the open bonnet, messed about with the engine for some time and—hey presto!—that damned jeep started. Were our faces red?

"That was my introduction to Bella Syms. There was another girl with her—Emily. Their farm was close by. They gave us a lunch of chicken, home-grown vegetables and home-made wine. It was the best damn meal we'd had for a long, long time. They wouldn't take anything, except our thanks. I didn't see them again until Emily applied for the post of music teacher which I'd advertised here, in Ceylon."

He paused. "I could hardly believe it was the same girl I'd seen in that Italian village, even allowing for the years. Of course, I gave her the job straightaway, and the house—"

"What were they doing in Ceylon?" asked Blake.

"They were born here. Their father was English—a tea planter in the Nuwara Eliya district. Their mother was a

Kandyan Sinhalese. She was a strikingly beautiful woman with a fair skin—I was shown the wedding photograph. Some of the Sinhalese in the hill country are quite fair, you know. Probably dates back to the time our forefathers were storming the hill capital, Kandy. Anyway, their mother died when the girls were quite small and the father went with an Italian friend to Italy, where he settled down and in time set up a farm. When he died the daughters took over. The Italians accepted them as one of themselves."

Heston got up and fetched another bottle of beer. "All this talking has made me thirsty," he apologised. "Will you have another?" Blake shook his head, and Heston filled his own mug and took a deep pull from it.

"Where was I? Oh yes, *les Syms filles*. Well, the girls were liked and respected and the Italian authorities didn't interfere with them even after Mussolini decided to team up with Hitler. The farm prospered but something must have happened shortly afterwards, and they closed up the farm and came back to Ceylon. I believe they had enough saved, but with their source of income no more and Bella an invalid, Emily decided to work. She's a first-class pianist and when she saw the advert—"

"What *is* the matter with Bella Syms?" asked Blake. "She is continually referred to as an invalid but, quite frankly, she appears to be in full possession of all her faculties, apart from having to use a hearing-aid. She is certainly not confined to a wheelchair—"

"I agree with you. Simply by looking at her you'd never think there was anything wrong. But she is reputed to have a weak heart and I rather think there's something up here—" Heston tapped his forehead. "The war affected many people that way. Perhaps Bella is another victim. You know, she sometimes thinks the war isn't yet over! And she's passionately on the side of the Allies. Have you seen her miniature battle-field?"

Blake nodded. "I have. I think I'll take another look at it. Besides, I told Paula I'd meet her there."

"I'll drive you down," offered Heston. "Half a mo' till I put some things on."

The coffee and Sexton Blake arrived simultaneously.

The sudden ring at the door startled Emily Syms so much that she almost dropped the cup in Paula's lap. Paula adroitly relieved her of the cup and saucer in one swift movement.

Bella said: "Emily dear, do be careful! Go and see who is at the door."

Emily obeyed and Bella smiled indulgently, rather like an understanding mother towards a child who is frightened of the dark, Paula thought.

"Drink your coffee, my dear."

Paula lifted the cup to her lips but before she could drink the door opened and Sexton Blake came in.

He wasn't alone. Behind him came other callers. Paula's eyes widened as she saw them. She set the cup down beside her and half-rose.

Emily Syms came fluttering behind Blake. She was hardly able to speak for excitement.

"Oh, Bella dear!" she burbled breathlessly. "It's Mr Blake again! And the others—"

"Do sit down, Mr Blake," said Bella. "I was just having a little chat with your secretary. Such a courageous girl! That leg must be very painful—"

She stared searchingly at the expanse of long slim leg and rounded thigh and Paula shifted a little uncomfortably. There was something more than disapproval in the woman's stare, she thought. As she moved her leg she accidentally kicked over the cup of coffee.

"Oh dear, I'm so sorry—" she began, but Bella's gaze had shifted and nobody seemed to have noticed the accident. In any case, Paula told herself, the coffee couldn't do much harm to the dingy-coloured carpet.

Blake had moved towards the objects on the sideboard. "This is a truly interesting collection you have, Miss Syms," he said. "I didn't really have time to look at it properly yesterday, but—" He moved closer. "May I examine it more closely now?"

"Of course!" said Bella, with evident pleasure. She rose majestically and moved towards the sideboard which stood in the confined space behind the sofa. Paula and Emily joined her, followed by the other guests.

"Please don't touch anything!" Bella warned. Proudly she explained the significance of every object on the miniature battlefield. Of them all Blake was the most interested.

When she had finished he said: "Thank you, Miss Syms. I wouldn't have missed this for anything."

Her eyes glowed. "You're too kind, Mr Blake. I'm not quite up to date with the news, I'm afraid. I'm sure you know more about what is going on. Won't you sit down?"

"You must excuse this intrusion," said Blake as they sorted themselves out. "I must take the blame since I took the liberty of inviting them here. You know them all, of course."

Emily clapped her hands and rocked to and fro in the ancient chair.

"Such a cosy, friendly gathering," she said. "We've never had so many visitors before." Then a troubled expression came into her eyes. "If only those two poor dear girls, and Mr Miller could have been with us—"

Paula glanced around at the now silent group of people sitting in the high-backed chairs. They were all there—Heston in an unbuttoned shirt hastily thrust into a pair of crumpled white trousers; Allen, as dapper as ever except for a large piece of sticking plaster on his forehead; Mary Floyd, still wan-faced and heavy-eyed, Eva Miller—

Paula wondered why Sexton Blake had brought them all with him.

Then the answer burst on her.

He had brought them all together because he had solved the case.

CHAPTER XIX

Tracked Down

Thyself shall see the act:
For, as thou urgest justice, be assur'd
Thou shalt have justice, more than thou desir'st.
Shakespeare: *Merchant of Venice.*

SEXTON BLAKE cleared his throat. Everybody looked at him expectantly. He stood in front of the empty fireplace, his hands thrust casually into his trouser pockets, his broad shoulders held back, his lean, aesthetic face set in firm lines. He said, without preamble:

"The murderer amongst us is, of course, one of you."

He waited until the ripple of excitement had died away.

The effect of his statement was as though he had dropped a bomb amongst them. There was absolute silence for a moment, then everybody started talking at the same time. Blake waved a hand for silence.

"If you don't mind, I'll have no more interruptions." He looked slowly from one face to the other—Bella, tight-lipped and obviously disapproving; Emily, open-mouthed; Mary Floyd, sad-eyed and watchful; Heston, tense and perspiring, his shirt soaked with sweat; Allen, goggle-eyed; Paula alert and eager.

"We'll start with the first murder—that of Eddie Vance," began Blake. "It has been established that Eddie left his house in the early hours of Saturday morning. Conrad Miller, his stepfather, heard the telephone ring and noted the time—one a.m. He thought Eddie had gone to meet a friend; he often went out at odd hours and everybody living in the lane must have been aware of this.

"Somebody made use of that knowledge to lure Eddie out and kill him. There then remained the question of the disposal of his body. The killer went across the road, took Allen's car from under the porch and put the body in the rear. The Anglia has a remarkably silent engine and Allen looked after his car very carefully.

"The killer—whom, for the present, I'll call 'X'—drove down towards the rail tracks—but not to leave the body there to be run over by a train. It was important at this juncture that Eddie should 'disappear'—to set the scene for Angela's murder. So he was rolled in the wire mesh—so opportunely provided by Allen—and dumped in the sea.

"Then the killer drove the Anglia back under Allen's porch and returned home.

"Now we come to the murder of Angela Floyd. According to the evidence of Miss Emily Syms, corroborated by several of her pupils, Judy Floyd was in the habit of leaving the classroom, ostensibly to go to the lavatory, at 10.25 each morning. She had started doing this shortly after the arrival of Eddie Vance. But she did not visit the lavatory, as she pretended to do—but climbed the mango tree in the school compound. I found marks on the tree and corresponding marks on the shoes she wore to school and which I examined at her home. She climbed the tree—not to pick mangoes—but to spy on her sister.

"I climbed the tree myself and saw that from a certain point the sun porch of every house in the lane—except, of course, this one, which had none—is visible. I also found marks which indicated that the particular bough which afforded this viewpoint had been used quite often, and recently.

"Who was the only person left in the lane when the others had gone to work? Angela Floyd. And for the past three weeks there had been Eddie. Within a week of his arrival he and Angela had become very friendly—more than friendly, perhaps—and they had a morning tryst at 10.30. Judy discovered this and took to watching them. On this particular day she would have seen something else. She not only witnessed the murder, but recognised the killer. But we'll return to that later.

"X arrived at the house at the time when Angela was expecting Eddie—undoubtedly the door had been left open for him. X was able to take Angela completely by surprise and beat her to death. The killer was now faced with the problem of getting back home without being seen by Allen, now working on his car. This must have presented an unexpected problem, for the killer had naturally believed the lane to be deserted. But that trip at night had almost drained away what little petrol had remained in Allen's car, unknown to Allen, who was looking for a mechanical fault why the Anglia wouldn't start.

"X hung around the house, waiting for Allen to go, but before he could trace the fault in his car, Allen heard the crows screaming and came running to the house. X dodged through the rear door as Allen came through the front, then ran along behind the hedge, parallel with the lane, to cross the road again lower down and get home without being seen.

"Next, X killed Conrad Miller. We knew how it was done—but not *why* it was done. As I pointed out to Vandebona, Miller could not possibly, even unwittingly, have come upon anything that could make him a security risk to X. Obviously the four murders were linked—so how did Miller fit into the general pattern?

"Then came the threat from Judy. X did not know it was Judy, for she had taken care to compose her ultimatum with letters cut from a book in Allen's study. She was alone for some hours in Allen's house on the night Miller died. There were traces of gum on Allen's writing table and I found the book which had contained the cut-out letters in his bookshelf when I searched the house early this morning, after the attack on him. X, not knowing the note was from Judy, made preparations to deal with an adult. And Judy, despite her air pistol, was an easy victim.

"But something happened last night which, like Miller's death, seemed at the time to be totally unconnected with the pattern of murder. Last night Allen's transmitter was destroyed. It appeared to be an act of senseless, wanton destruction—but there must have been a good reason for it."

He paused, looking almost unseeingly at the group before him.

"So, you see, there are four main questions to be answered: One, why was Eddie Vance killed? Two, why was Angela Floyd killed? Three, why was Conrad Miller killed? And four—why was the radio transmitter smashed?"

Blake went on: "Before we come to the answers to those questions it is necessary to point out that any one of you could have committed the murders. Only Miller had a real alibi, backed by independent witnesses who saw him in a bar between 10.05 and 10.25 on the day Angela was murdered.

"I even considered the possibility that there could have been two murderers. Miller was interested in Angela Floyd—and could have killed Eddie during a moment of overwhelming jealousy when he heard Eddie take the phone call and thought he was going out to meet Angela. On the other hand, he could not have killed Angela. But Eva Miller could have done, obsessed with hatred of the girl who had "trapped" her son, to whom she was devoted.

"Heston could have killed both Eddie and Angela—Eddie because, like Miller, he was jealous of him, and Angela because she repulsed his advances. Likewise Allen. Subsequently Miller and Judy were killed—the apparent motive for Miller's murder being that he accidentally stumbled on something dangerous to X; while Judy had to be killed because she knew too much.

"There was another person who could have killed Angela. That person had no alibi—and also had the opportunity to kill not only Angela but the others. Miss Emily Syms—" He looked at Emily, who started so violently that she set the rocking-chair rocking alarmingly.

"But, Mr Blake—" Emily's voice rose on a high falsetto note.

Blake glanced from her to Bella. "And the same goes for you too, Miss Bella—"

Then, suddenly, the doorbell rang.

At a sign from Blake, Paula went to open the door. She returned followed by Inspector Vandebona.

Vandebona's eyes widened in surprise at sight of the little tableau.

"I'm glad you got my message, Inspector," Blake said briefly. "Please take a seat. I was explaining to these people how each one of them had the opportunity—and in some cases the motive—to commit the murders. Let us now go back to the beginning, for there are other questions which arise.

"We know that X took Eddie's body in Allen's car, taking care to leave no prints on it—"

"But *how* did he take my car?" demanded Allen. "I always keep it locked. It was locked that night—"

"You're sure about that? You didn't leave the key in the ignition?"

"No. I'll swear I didn't. I never fail to lock the car last thing at night—"

"And where do you leave your keys, including the ignition key?"

"On my dressing-table upstairs. They were there in the morning."

Blake looked at him thoughtfully. "Then, as the car had not been tampered with, somebody obviously had a duplicate key."

Allen looked stunned.

"This means," said Blake, "that X had planned Eddie's murder in advance, and knew exactly how to carry it out. A duplicate key could—and was—obtained quite easily.

"We will now consider another question. It has been established that Eddie and Angela met regularly at 10.30, as soon as they judged the "coast was clear" for their tryst. X came at the exact time Angela was expecting Eddie; in other words, the killer knew exactly when to come.

"The killer also brought the murder weapon—an iron bar, which proves beyond doubt that the murder was premeditated. It would also appear to rule out Allen and Heston—a man does not normally approach a girl in order to make advances to her, armed with an iron bar! It could have been, of course, that after being repulsed the killer left the house, grabbed up the iron bar, and returned to kill Angela. But this seems hardly likely—and Floyd stated there was no such iron bar anywhere in the house. X could hardly have returned home, chosen a weapon, and gone back to kill Angela. Don't forget the crows! They were on the scene within minutes of Angela's death.

"Judy had been spying on her sister and Eddie—and so had the murderer. And who, apart from Judy, when all the others had left, would be in a position to do so, watching the girl and Eddie as they made love on the sun porch?"

Blake's voice was still conversational as he turned to Bella. "It was you who purloined Jeffrey Floyd's binoculars, wasn't it, Miss Syms?"

Almost before Blake had finished speaking, before the others could take in the stunning implication of his words, Bella Syms had moved.

She moved with surprising speed. She hurled herself from her chair, treading hard on the curved end of the rocking chair.

The chair rose sharply. With a terrified shriek Emily Syms sailed through the air and alighted in a tangle of voluminous underwear on the luckless Allen. The force of the impact sent Allen's chair skidding backwards along the floor. It came to rest against the what-not and Allen and Emily both vanished beneath an avalanche of crashing crockery.

Heston jumped aside and cannoned into Vandebona. Blake and Paula made a simultaneous rush forward, but the flying skirts of Emily impeded them.

Suddenly it was too late.

Bella was covering them with a deadly-looking Mauser which she had whipped from the pocket of her long, flowing skirt.

"Keep your distance, Mr Blake. And the rest of you. Keep your hands where I can see them. And don't move. If you do, I shall shoot. I'm a pretty good shot and I can't possibly miss at this range. I might get more than one of you before you could possibly overpower me.

"I'm not bluffing. The gun is loaded. I found it on a German, in Italy, after I had killed him. I killed him by hitting him on the head with a rock—you see, he was trying to rape Emily. That's why she claims to owe me so much; why she's always been grateful to me.

"I'm glad you are all being sensible. I must be going soon, but I'm sure Mr Blake will be disappointed if I don't answer his questions. Yes, I *was* spying on that shameless girl. This house, as you have observed, is high-roofed and from the dormer windows in the attic where I sometimes go to meditate I could see right into the sun porch of the Floyd's house. At first I thought my eyes were deceiving me—they are not too good over a long distance, and this house is well back from the road. So I found an opportunity to take Mr Floyd's binoculars. After all, it was in a good cause. They confirmed my worst suspicions.

"Angela Floyd and that young man! The things I saw them do! I should be ashamed even to mention them. And it went on day after day. Their sins called to Heaven for punishment. I knew then that I had been made an instrument of divine vengeance. For, as the good Book says, 'thus were they defiled with their own works and went a-whoring with their own inventions'."

"Now I realised my true mission in life. It was given to me to smite the sinner and the ungodly. I knew it for certain when Mrs Miller called to tell me about Eddie's disappearance and Angela's death—and I learned from her that Miller was a German. That is why I killed him. There would be one German less for England and her allies to deal with.

"I had to kill Judy Floyd, though I was somewhat grieved about this; in fact it has worried me considerably. For does not the Bible say that 'whoso shall offend one of these little ones, it were better that a millstone were hanged about his neck and that he were drowned in the depth of the sea?' But she knew too much—and if she had told what she knew it would have impeded me in my work. Also, she tried to blackmail me, which was ungodly and deserving of punishment.

"Then you arrived, Mr Blake, and I was seriously perturbed. I had a feeling you could not be fooled, as I had succeeded in fooling the police. So last night I attempted to eliminate both you and Miss Dane, here. I failed although I succeeded in one thing—I destroyed the radio which that renegade Englishman, that traitor—" She gestured towards the dumfounded Allen "—had in his house. I had been aware for some time that he was transmitting intelligence to the German High Command —Heaven alone knows what harm he has done to the Allies!

"When I got back home, however, there was a shock awaiting me. A man I had never seen before. He had witnessed my attack on Miss Dane and attempted to blackmail me. I dealt with him, of course. He had letters on him which said his name was Freddie de Soysa—"

She intercepted the startled look which Paula flung at Blake. Freddie the Frightful, the Walton wolf! It was the last name Paula had expected to hear.

Bella was backing slowly towards the door, still keeping the gun trained upon her silent audience. Nobody moved. Paula shot a glance at Blake. She knew that if he had been on his own he would have chanced hurling himself at the demented woman and wresting the gun from her, but he could not take that chance when it meant risking the lives of his companions. Undoubtedly she would fire at the first hostile movement.

Bella looked suddenly at Mary Floyd. "Oh, by the way, Mrs Floyd, you might be interested to know that your husband is here," she said dispassionately. "He came early this morning with some foolish idea of hiding in my house while he made his own investigations into the death of his daughters. Of course, the situation would have been impossible. I had to take care of him—"

Mary swayed and every last vestige of blood drained from

her cheeks. "Jeffrey!" she gasped. "You—you murderess! Isn't it enough that you killed my children—"

"Silence!" said Bella sternly. "I've no further time to waste on you. I must be going."

"How far do you think you'll get?" asked Blake smoothly. "You can't possibly escape, Miss Bella, and you know it."

She looked at him and now there was animosity in her eyes. "You, Mr Blake, have been a thorn in my side," she said. "As the Book says, if thine eye offends thee, pluck it out. Before I leave this house I am afraid I shall have to shoot you. There is still a great deal I have to do and I cannot allow you to constantly impede me."

She was standing at the foot of the stairs and the muzzle of the deadly-looking weapon had swung to cover Blake. Paula, in horror, heard the click of the released hammer and choked back a gasp. The others stood white-faced, as though frozen into stone. Only Blake showed no emotion. His face was bland, almost relaxed, but Paula knew that behind those grey eyes his brain was working at lightning speed.

There was a faint movement from the top of the stairs. The hearing-aid had slipped from Bella's ear and dangled at the end of its cord, and she heard nothing. She stood with her back to the staircase and now the vicious Mauser was centred in a direct line with Blake's heart.

The trigger finger tightened. And in that second Jeffrey Floyd, standing at the top of the staircase, catapulted himself through the air with the velocity of a thunderbolt and struck her fairly and squarely between the shoulders, bringing her to the floor.

Bella fell heavily, with Floyd on top of her. But as he rolled over she leapt to her feet with astonishingly cat-like agility and fired. The bullet cut along the side of his head and he fell back, his face a mask of blood.

Blake and Paula sprang forward, but Emily, screaming on a high, hysterical note, stumbled in front of them. Heston, in his haste, barked his shin against a heavy chair and pulled up short, cursing. Vandebona almost fell over the stooping Heston. Allen stood where he was, too stupefied to move.

By the time Blake had clambered past the clawing Emily the figure of Bella was at the outer door. She opened it, pausing to fire at Blake. The bullet went wide, smashing a wall mirror. Blake reached the door, with Paula close behind him.

Heston's car was drawn up outside and Bella was already grabbing at the handle of the driving-seat door. She wrenched it open and scrambled behind the wheel; a second later the engine started up.

As Blake rushed forward she leaned through the open window and hurled the gun at him. It struck him on the shoulder and dropped to the ground. The car swept down the drive; at the gate she suddenly turned the car to the left, then stopped with a squeal of brakes and hurriedly backed. She changed into first with a terrific crashing of gears and wheeled the car to the right.

Blake made a flying grab for the boot handle but missed. The car sped down towards the rail tracks. He continued his rush into the lane.

Then he realised why Bella had changed course. Coming down the road was Melder's car. There was no room in the narrow lane for the A55 and the Humber to pass.

The Humber drew abreast of Blake and he flung himself into it. "Go on!" he snapped. "After her!"

The Humber jerked forward in pursuit. Bella had had a good start, but Blake was confident that he could catch up with her. The lane was a cul-de-sac; Bella would have to continue her flight on foot.

"Hurry, man!" he urged. He had the door open, ready to jump out. Now the A55 had reached the end of the lane. Bella sprang out. He caught a fleeting glimpse of her face, rage-distorted, as she looked back. Then she was running towards the tracks. If she continued along the footpath beside the ballast she could make her way to the next lane; there might be a car there, if her luck held good.

Blake didn't wait for the Humber to stop. He flung himself

out, landing lightly with his knees bent and at the same moment he started running.

Bella looked back again. He saw her face, wild in the sunshine.

He put everything he had into a terrific burst of speed. Bella was running clumsily along the cinder-strewn footpath, her skirt ballooning in the breeze from the sea.

Blake reached the footpath. He had narrowed the gap and now only about three hundred yards separated them. He knew he could catch up with her within minutes.

Bella also seemed to realise it. She kicked away her flat-heeled shoes and sprang onto the sleepers. That way she could make faster progress.

Blake kept going along the footpath, the cinders crunching under his flying feet. Behind him he thought he heard Melder shout, but he couldn't be sure because of the roar of the sea.

He was astonished at the turn of speed Bella was showing. For a self-professed invalid she was doing remarkably well! His guess that she was in full possession of all her faculties had been right; beneath that sagging flesh was a deceptively masked strength.

Then, from behind him, he heard a sudden rumbling noise. Just in time he flung himself aside. He yelled a warning, but the giant slipstream of the train hurled the words away.

He had a glimpse of Bella's face as she looked back momentarily. He saw the terror on it, and her vain attempt to leap clear. That was the last he saw of her—alive and in one piece.

The train ground to a halt, but too late. The hiss of the vacuum and escaping steam mingled with the roar of the sea. The sun blazed down on all that remained of Bella Syms—a heap of twisted, blood-soaked rags with scarcely anything left in them of humanity.

CHAPTER XX

Epitaph to Evil

He who does evil that good may come
pays a toll to the devil to let him into heaven.
J. C. and A. W. Hare: *Guesses at Truth.*

EMILY SYMS was crying, her thin body shaking with gusts of grief. Eva Miller sat beside her, a large hand round the bent shoulders, trying to comfort her.

"Come now, Emily, pull yourself together. It's all over now . . ."

Emily blew her nose into a large handkerchief.

"Oh, how dreadful it's all been!" she sobbed. "To think that Bella could have been so wicked. She always seemed so righteous, preaching the love of God and quoting from the Bible. In fact, religion was almost a mania with her—"

"It *was* a mania with her," said Blake. "That was the root of the whole trouble. She finally saw herself as the instrument of divine retribution. And what made her doubly dangerous was her distorted patriotism. She believed that the war wasn't yet over, that all Germans were enemies. From the moment she killed that German, in Naples, her whole nature must have changed. She was filled with an unreasoning hatred of Germans—and of sex. Of anything connected with sex, in fact. In the end it became an obsession."

Emily looked up. She said shakily. "That's the reason we came back here. Killing that German did something to her; she changed completely. I think she was always a little mad.

She got it into her head that she was fighting the war practically singlehanded; that it was her duty to destroy the enemy at all costs. In the end I got her to sell the farm and we came here; I thought she would perhaps get better once we were away from those things that reminded her. And she really did seem to improve. She would spend hours with that miniature battlefield, staging mock battles, killing the Germans over and over again. It seemed to release something in her. And then—"

"And then she saw Eddie and Angela together," said Blake. "Perhaps she was reminded again of the scene between the German and her sister. At any rate, a part of her crazed brain resolved to kill them."

He went on: "After that, there was no stopping her. She had a reason—or believed she had a reason—for killing Eddie and Angela, even Judy. But when she killed Conrad Miller she had ceased to reason. She imagined herself surrounded by the 'enemy'—myself, Paula, Allen, the supposed traitor. Even Freddie de Soysa—that misguided, would-be blackmailer— was an enemy, to be outwitted, outsmarted, and destroyed."

Paula shuddered. In the attic from which Jeffrey Floyd had so providentially escaped they had found what remained of poor Freddie—after the rats had dealt with him. Paula had clambered up the short step-ladder into the attic before Blake could stop her and had come down at precipitate speed, her stomach heaving.

In the attic Blake and Vandebona had also found the murder weapon—the short iron bar with which Bella had struck down her victims. It was caked with blood and matted with hair; a grim and grisly thing which Blake had hurriedly concealed from the sight of the others.

"One thing puzzles me, chief," Paula had said, when she had sufficiently recovered from her momentary sickness. "How on earth did Bella get Freddie and Jeffrey Floyd into the attic? She could hardly have pushed them up the ladder—or carried them over her shoulder."

"I think she heaved them up in the same way a miller might

heave up a sack of grain," said Blake. "We found a length of strong rope in the attic, slung over a cross-beam directly in line with the trapdoor. I imagine she tied the rope around Freddie's body—and Floyd—as they lay immediately under the open trapdoor of the attic, threw the other end of the rope over the cross-beam, and hauled them up. Even so, it was no mean feat for a woman—"

"She must have been tremendously strong," said Paula. "Apart from getting them into the attic, she must have had to drag them upstairs. And," she added grimly, "not content with killing poor Freddie, she tried to poison *me*!"

She remembered the spilt cup of coffee. On their return to the house she had noticed the dark patch against the sofa, surrounded by a number of flies. And the flies were dead!

"You had a narrow escape, Paula—I should have said *another* narrow escape," said Blake. "I blame myself for not having warned you that Bella might be the person we were seeking. But I had no idea, of course, that her madness had reached such proportions."

"I can't believe it even now," said Mary Floyd shakily. "'Bella, of all people! She seemed so... harmless. And now my two girls are dead, and Jeffrey—" She glanced at Floyd, standing at her side, still covered with the dust and dirt from the attic, his face streaked with blood from the gash along his temple "—I might have lost Jeffrey too."

"It was my own fault," muttered Floyd. "I should have left things to Blake. But how could I possibly guess the truth about that monstrous woman? If I'd known before I'd have strangled her with my bare hands—"

"How did you come to suspect her, chief?" asked Paula.

"The murder of Angela Floyd gave me a pointer," he said. "It was not a sex crime in the strict sense of the term. That was significant considering the motives attributed to Eddie Vance, Heston and Allen. She had been beaten to death with savage fury by someone who had kept on hitting her long after she was dead. It looked like the work of a maniac—but not a sex maniac; there had been no attempt at criminal assault. It could have been a woman; a woman with manic tendencies fired by sex. That was Pointer No 1.

"Pointer No 2 was the fact that Angela had been killed at the time she was expecting Eddie—and whoever killed her knew the time of the tryst. My suspicions focused on Bella and Emily, but Emily could not have been spying from the music class with the children around her—besides, the wall facing the lane is windowless. So that left Bella.

"Pointer No 3 was that the house is high-roofed and has dormer windows overlooking the sun porch of the Floyd house. Bella Syms was alone there in the mornings, with plenty of time to spare.

"Pointer No 4 was Emily's headache on the morning Angela was killed. Had she been drugged the previous night to leave the coast clear for Bella? The same thing happened last night, when Bella left the house to deal with Allen's transmitter—and attacked Paula and myself.

"Pointer No 5 was that the key to the front door of this house was with Emily. She used it to unlock the door and let me in then she immediately locked it again. I checked and found there was no way out except through the front door. Bella made a point of telling me that the locks and bolts were for the purpose of keeping the 'enemy' out. We now know from Emily that on the day Angela was murdered she found the front door unlocked. She did not mention this to Vandebona—through loyalty to her sister, or perhaps even fear of her—but Bella sensed that she was puzzled and taxed her about it the following day. She convinced Emily that she must have made a mistake; that she had forgotten to lock the front door herself.

"You remember Emily told me that twice during their weekly trips to the Pettah, Bella 'disappeared'? I made inquiries and found that she had obtained duplicates of the front door key and of the ignition key of Allen's car. The locksmith remembered her quite clearly.

"Pointer No 6 was given this morning by Mary Floyd when she remembered her husband's missing binoculars. They were hidden in the attic. There is no doubt that Bella used the dormer windows as observation posts."

Emily shivered. "She was often up there, I know. She knew I would never set foot in the attic. Those rats!" She buried her face in her hands again.

Blake went on: "But what puzzled me—and in a sense laid a red-herring across the trail—was Miller's death. It just didn't seem to fit in with the other murders. That was why, for a time, I even considered the possibility that we had *two* killers at large. Then Mrs Miller and Heston gave me the final pointers this morning—Mrs Miller when she told me of her husband's German origin and Heston when he mentioned Bella's obsessional hatred of Germans. That, coupled with the grim game she continued to play with her miniature battlefield, substantiated my belief. Miller was a German by birth.

"Then there was the incident of the jeep in Italy, which Heston mentioned to me. Bella had considerable knowledge of motor mechanics—she was able to put right a fault which none of the soldiers could find. It would have been easy for her to tamper with the brakes on Miller's car.

"As soon as the truth struck me—the identity of 'X'—I gathered you all together and brought you here. I intended to take Bella off-guard by casting suspicion on each of you in turn. But I was perhaps over-confident—I did not realise she would be carrying a gun. Things might have turned out tragically for some of us if Floyd had not so providently escaped."

Floyd nodded soberly. "I've got that poor devil, Freddie de Soysa, to thank for that. When I came to in that black hell-hole and heard the rats—well, I honestly thought it was curtains. And I got the fright of my life when he touched me. He was half-dead even then—in fact, those bloody rats had already been nibbling at him—but he managed to loosen one of the knots before he finally passed out. It took him hours—and it took me as long again to free myself. By that time he was already dead. I crept out of the attic, meaning to take Bella by surprise—in fact, all I wanted to do was get my hands around her throat and squeeze the life out of her—then I heard voices. I listened, realised what was happening and . . . Well, the rest you know."

He looked at Mary Floyd, put his arm around her shoulders. "Now that this is all cleared up, darling, we'll go away from this dreadful place," he said. "I never want to see Ceylon again."

She nodded, wordlessly, reaching up to grip his hand.

Sexton Blake got up and moved towards the door, with Paula at his heels. The ambulance had just departed, taking what was left of Freddie de Soysa. Now the others were preparing to return to their respective homes.

"What about Emily?" asked Paula. "It doesn't seem right to leave her here by herself."

Blake gave a weary shrug of his shoulders. "Let that be somebody else's problem," he said. He looked up at the blazing sun and in spite of the heat he felt a chill go through him. Tomorrow, thank God, he would be back in England, under its leaden skies.

"And I hope it's raining," he said as he and Paula went slowly down the weed-grown drive together.

Paula did not reply, but she looked up and gave him an understanding smile. She did not have to ask him what he meant, for she already knew. She felt exactly the same way herself.

THE END